GOD'S SCOREKEEPER
and Other Stories

GOD'S SCOREKEEPER
and Other Stories

Frank G. Honeycutt

CASCADE *Books* · Eugene, Oregon

GOD'S SCOREKEEPER AND OTHER STORIES

Cascade Books
An Imprint of Wipf and Stock Publishers
199 W. 8th Ave., Suite 3
Eugene, OR 97401

www.wipfandstock.com

PAPERBACK ISBN: 978-1-5326-7551-5
HARDCOVER ISBN: 978-1-5326-7552-2
EBOOK ISBN: 978-1-5326-7553-9

Cataloguing-in-Publication data:

Names: Honeycutt, Frank G., author.

Title: God's scorekeeper and other stories / Frank G. Honeycutt.

Description: Eugene, OR: Cascade Books, 2019

Identifiers: ISBN 978-1-5326-7551-5 (paperback) | ISBN 978-1-5326-7552-2 (hardcover) | ISBN 978-1-5326-7553-9 (ebook)

Subjects: LCSH: Clergy—Fiction. | Humorous stories, American.

Classification: PS3568.03125 G556 2019 (print) | PS3568.03125 (ebook)

Manufactured in the U.S.A.   AUGUST 20, 2019

For John Gifford and Michael Kohn

Excellent Friends
Faithful Readers
Angular Inspiration

Contents

Acknowledgments

THIS COLLECTION OF STORIES describing rather unusual pastors would not be possible without the love, inspiration, and support of the congregations I've served in a ministry spanning three decades:

St. Paul and Trinity Lutheran Churches
Stephens City, Virginia

St. John Lutheran Church
Abingdon, Virginia

Ebenezer Lutheran Church
Columbia, South Carolina

St. John's Lutheran Church
Walhalla, South Carolina

I'd also like to thank the following kind folk who read and responded to first drafts of the stories: John Gifford, Michael Kohn, Cindy Honeycutt, Nancy Tuten, Paul Pingel, Tina and Howard Pillot, Andy Coone, John Hoffmeyer, Ron Luckey, Ken Robbins, Micky and Tom Ward, Paul Wilson, Mark McLean, Dan Shonka, Peggy and Kent Oehm, Dean Floyd, John Lang, Larry Harley, Ed Davis, Martha Reiser Williams, John Dooley, Chris Heavner, and my three children who've put up with lots over the years from their dad, an odd pastor—Hannah, Marta, and Lukas.

Acknowledgments

I'm indebted to Rodney Clapp (my editor at Brazos and Cascade) for encouragement and expert guidance. Thanks, Rodney.

I am grateful to note here that the sixth story in this collection, "Pastor Polar," won first place in fiction at the 2019 Porter Fleming Literary Competition, at the Morris Museum of Art, in Augusta, Georgia.

Finally, I'd be remiss not to mention gratitude for my fellow Whiskey Theologians, Tom and Chris, whose campfire insights have sparked and corralled many unhinged ideas.

The Emperor of Embellishment

UNDETECTED BY THE GOLFERS above him on the elevated seventh tee, a diminutive bespectacled man with a Braves cap and shoulder pouch crawls on hands and knees, completely hidden, through a ravine of twisting vines and thick rhododendron. The pouch resembles those carried by walking mailmen, even though the little pastor mostly slithers like a studious and searching snake. His long-sleeved canvas shirt has patches on both elbows, still protecting him after years of happy hunts from thorn scratches and yellow jacket stings.

In his pouch rest ninety-seven lost golf balls, including a few gleaming Titleists and Callaways whose appearances suggest only recent removal from new sleeves of three—flubbed tee shots which have found their way via gravity and colorful cursing into the vegetative hazard dubbed "Satan's Seacoast Hideaway" by Mexican grounds keepers at Mountain Glen Country Club. Crawling, peering, and finding, Pastor Bill often wonders about this odd designation hundreds of miles from any South Carolina beach.

Bill takes a break from his links labors, looks up at the sky on his back through the tangled laurel branches, and smiles at the various theological intersections between leading a sometimes wayward church flock and finding lost golf balls. The Bible says that Jesus left ninety-nine to search for a single lost sheep. To honor the power and punch of the story, Bill usually pauses just before reaching the century mark to reflect upon his years of service as a pastor, often spent looking for wayward lives resembling errant tee shots lost among the weeds.

He closes his eyes for a couple minutes and soon hears the distinctive rattle of the beverage cart, braking down the steep descent into the ravine.

The pastor loudly whistles twice, a long trill and another short one. A young woman named Bridget—one of Bill's favorite former confirmation students now majoring in Biology at Clemson—stops the cart, retrieves a beer from the cooler, and hides the can in the tall grass bordering the concrete path. She will soon enter her sophomore year after a summer of earning cash from old men who don't mind parting with tens and even twenties if the golf is going well. Bridget pulls a harmonica from the pocket of her shorts and plays the first notes of "Amazing Grace" before continuing on towards the seventh green. Bill whistles back and knows a cold beverage will be nice after his sweaty search.

*

The pro at Mountain Glen, Rusty LeBleu, is a transplanted Louisianan who played college golf at LSU but could never quite secure his tour playing card at Q-School. After seven failed attempts, Rusty begrudgingly accepted the relative demotion of presiding over beginning range lessons, interactive tact and general comportment for the club's fleet of fetching cart girls, and even the daily menu for the small snack bar attractively wedged between the ninth and eighteenth greens.

Even at sixty, rain or shine, Rusty walks the entire course each morning with a two-iron, the perfect hiking staff for his still-lanky frame. He often narrates his only round at Augusta National for a cadre of young admirers who hang upon his every word.

"We had a tournament one April weekend in Atlanta against Georgia Tech and Auburn at the old East Lake Golf Club, a favorite, as I'm sure you lads know, of the immortal Bobby Jones. Yours truly, of course, was the medalist. I absolutely stuck my Sunday approach shot on sixteen, a long uphill par four, pin high, with this very club."

With nimble dexterity, Rusty twirled the club like a baton and then aimed the two-iron at a low-flying mallard, squeezing an imaginary trigger with two accompanying tongue-thwocks. "And brought those pussy college boys to their knees."

"You made the putt, didn't you?" asked a little boy whose golf cap with the Mountain Glen logo—a rusty setting sun under a pale blue sky, aptly matching the moniker of his proximate hero—barely reached the pro's rippling abdominal six-pack.

"Make it? Damn thing was practically a gimmee. I'm as accurate as Wyatt Earp with this old club. So, I holed out and then drained a sixty-footer from the far fringe just for show on a hundred dollar bet with this supposed whiz kid from Tech. Almost got me disqualified, but nobody messes with The Legend." The bevy of small boys looked up at Rusty with open mouths like a flock of baby birds waiting to be fed.

"That's actually the putt Chi-Chi Rodriguez saw on the evening news that weekend and got me invited to the '73 Masters two days later for a Tuesday practice round. He wanted a southerner to show him the Augusta ropes and keep him from wandering mesmerized into the azaleas with floral scents that reminded him of the gentle breezes of San Juan. I'd never been on the course but didn't tell the little man that. Sent my teammates back to Baton Rouge on the bus and rented a car at Chi-Chi's expense. The crazy little Puerto Rican finished tenth that year and I can't help but think my practice round (a sixty-eight from the tips) loosened him up for the nail-biting battle ahead. His best finish ever at The Masters, my young protégés. Now let's keep walking. It's pretty steep here, Timmy Tonnage, and I don't want you to cry to your momma if those extra pounds around your waist make you trip. So be careful."

The pack of boys laughed. They all looked back at Timothy Robertson, a nine-year-old who'd been bringing up the rear. He was crying under the bill of his cap, pulled low. No one noticed except the small man crouched and hidden in the dense undergrowth of the nearby woods. He said a quick prayer for the boy, then stood up and watched as the group walked up the dewy fourteenth fairway. A long pouch of golf balls hung loosely over his left shoulder.

*

That evening with his wife, Patty, Bill was watching Sheriff Andy Taylor smile broadly behind his desk, patiently instructing his hapless deputy whose zeal for reining in lawlessness had reached a fevered and comical pitch. Barney threw his police hat on the floor, again furiously outwitted, just as Opie came through the office door wearing his schoolboy innocence. Bill and Patty, both retired, enjoyed watching the Mayberry antics every weekday at seven on channel thirteen.

The predictable theme-whistling tune ended the show and Bill said, "You know the young Robertson boy from church?"

"Timothy? His parents divorced a couple years ago, right?"

"Yeah, cute kid. Could lose a bit of weight, but a nice young man. Rather innocent and sensitive. Opie made me think of him just now. I was glad to learn today that Timothy's taking golf lessons at the course, but I'm a little worried about that boy."

"I wondered how long it would take you to turn your ball-hunting hobby into some sort of ministry. Let me guess. You heard something salacious from one of your concealed hobbit holes. The ravine on number seven? Satan's Hellhole?"

"Seacoast Hideaway. Fools golfers into thinking even the devil takes a break. But no, the woods along the fourteenth fairway. Miguel and Tomas need to come up with a clever name for that wicked wedge of vicious vegetation." Bill still loved using alliteration even though he rarely preached anymore.

"I found 110 balls there this morning but paid for it." He pulled up the sleeve of his bathrobe and revealed a couple long scratches on his right arm.

"I'm assuming you paused at ninety-nine or thereabouts, right? Mr. Predictability. You need to retire that shirt."

"Never. It can be mended. Will you?"

Patty rolled her eyes. "I need to know what you plan to do with all the lost balls you so zealously find. I counted 9000 in the garage the other day. Ninety boxes of 100. I'm sure the kids will love finding those when it's time for their parents to move to assisted living. But tell me about Timothy."

"Two words. Rusty LeBleu."

"Ah. Not surprised."

One day at the turn in the snack bar with a foursome of pastors between the front and back nine, Bill invited Rusty, a lapsed Catholic, to worship at Good Shepherd Lutheran. Bridget, who flipped burgers at the club before she was promoted to the select team of cart girls, looked at her pastor wide-eyed through the order window as he extended the invitation.

Her boss was at the cash register, his back to Bridget. She shook her head and even tried to wave at Pastor Bill as Rusty said, "Well, thankee padre, as we used to say in the Loosiana Bye-yo. May just take you up on that. Think I've got a few unique blessings from The Big Guy known to no other man alive, you know?"

Rusty stuck out one arm and raised a leg in a life-size facsimile of the Heisman Trophy pose. "Might just pad your pews and swell your coffers. Hear you could use a little help over at Good Shep."

At the door of the church after worship on Rusty's first Sunday, Bridget waited for the line to clear. In a low voice she said, "I know you taught us in confirmation class that Jesus loves all people, but be sure to watch that one. He's gonna need a lot of love and forgiveness from somebody."

Bill glanced over Bridget's shoulder back into the nave. Rusty was regaling female members of the Lucy Derrick Circle with his latest golf exploit. A double eagle on the twelfth hole, a long par-five that Bill knew even Jesus could never reach in two.

*

Bill missed parts of being a pastor at times but had to admit to Patty (and others when they asked) that he did not miss the regular conflicts and tension that went with the job. Confronting somebody about their marital infidelity or just being a general Christian jackass always took a toll.

The pastoral headache surrounding Rusty LeBleu took a bit of time to surface. Rusty joined the property committee, a natural for a guy with grounds maintenance expertise, and quickly worked his way up to chair the all-male group. Bill sat in on some of the committee meetings to provide pastoral counsel but couldn't attend them all. Even in retirement, Bill still regretted missing one key meeting.

After a brief opening devotional soliciting thoughts about what club in the golf bag would have been Jesus' favorite had he played the game in Galilee, Rusty floated a fundraising idea among the group of men who were meeting one warm Thursday evening in spring in the youth room on the church's second floor.

"Yeah, I know all that about our Lord's anger at the moneychangers that day in the temple, but these are dire times, gentlemen. And if Saint Peter could've laced a Big Bertha driver like yours truly then I doubt the J-man would have needed that kid's fish and chips to feed the 5000. He could've just had the whole thing catered. We have a mortgage to pay and you're looking at your new Savior, lads. Follow me."

The men laughed, nervously, as they followed Rusty up the rickety stairs to the church clock tower in the last light of the day. They admired the mechanical innards of the ancient timepiece—which still required manual winding by a team of much younger men than these—forged by a German clockmaker just prior to the Civil War. They all knew the clock set off blaring gongs at the top of each hour, the sonorous tones echoing to the

5

far reaches of the town line, but rather deafening up close. Rusty had fifteen minutes to explain his idea before risking the ire of several wives who would undoubtedly show up at the course the next morning, complaining about their husbands' ruined hearing aids. Rusty spoke quickly, like a small child on Christmas morning.

"Few know about this secret porch just to the right of the clock face." He opened a screen window, disturbed a wasp nest, and received a sting on his left elbow.

"Sheee-it!"

A mother strolling her infant on the sidewalk below looked up, a bit surprised that such a word emanated from the holy and historic structure. "Sorry, ma'am!" Rusty yelled down. "Just got nipped by one of Satan's vermin."

The men inside the tower laughed. Rusty had them in the palm of his hand. He was now standing on a little ledge barely wide enough for the person who maintained the hour and minute hands each spring and fall when the time changed.

"You see the post office there in the distance?" The men gathered around the window, wide enough for three heads to poke out, on the opposite side of the clockface. "The idea here is to tee-up my trusty driver on this little porch and take bets on whether I can smack a gleaming Pro-V1 Titleist over the top of the post office and into Miz Myrtle Wilson's back yard, with her permission of course. What would you say the distance from here to there might be, Wally? About 350 yards?"

Wally Benson was eighty now, the former club champion at Mountain Glen. "Every bit of that, I'd say. But remember the wind often comes at us from the direction of the post office. That could be some wallop."

"All the better," said Rusty. "In Loosiana as a teenager, I smacked a ball over our backyard bye-yo teeming with snapping gators using my daddy's prize Maxfli, his winning ball at the Southern Amateur in 1962. Won ten dollars from a buddy. But the real risk of *not* making the distance was the possibility of diving for that lost ball rather than face my daddy's belt. Bring on the wind, no problem. This could make us some money for the church, fellas. Whaddya say?"

Without Pastor Bill's knowledge, out of town that week for some needed rest after Holy Week and Easter, a Saturday morning in May dawned with an impressive crowd of people gathered on the church sidewalk. Police stopped traffic for thirty minutes as the spectacle built in intensity.

The church chimes gonged ten times. Five minutes later, 300 faces looked up towards the clock at a grinning man armed with a bucket of golf balls and a Big Bertha driver. Rusty acknowledged their applause with a single tip of his LSU golf cap. Wally Benson sat at a long church table borrowed from the fellowship hall. He and the rest of the property committee men sold tickets and breakfast pastries, taking bets on the side. Rusty warmed up for no more than sixty seconds with a variety of impressive stretches (especially for a shelf-like deck with the floor dimensions of a small closet) and teed up the first ball. The crowd hushed, just like on television, as property committee members raised signs that read "Quiet, Please."

The first five balls—hoisted in triumph upon safe landing by Myrtle Wilson's grandson, Johnny, and broadcast with a wild-game camera back to a bank of televisions on the church lawn with only a five-second delay—cleared the post office easily. Each successful shot produced roars of approval from the happy throng who continued to pass various sums of cash (and the occasional personal check) to Wally and his smiling cohorts. Rusty reached his hand inside the clockface window and switched on a tape player that boomed "Nearer My God to Thee" through specially placed speakers on the church grounds. Rusty thought this might heighten the incentive for the crowd to part with even more cash. He was right.

The sixth tee shot started out well, despite a lower trajectory than the first five. But a chilly spring breeze from Table Rock, shining gloriously in the distance over the peak of the post office, doomed the drive soon after it left Rusty's club. The gleaming Titleist smacked a large hemlock tree with a resounding thud, ricocheted back across Main Street on the fly and crashed through a stained glass window depicting Jesus the Shepherd cradling a small baby lamb.

*

Shortly after the wily Ernest T. Bass again embarrassed Deputy Barney Fife with crafty elusiveness and unpredictably wise hillbilly lunacy, Bill turned off the television and said, "I know this doesn't sound like sane pastoral behavior, but I'm hatching a prank to give that cocky golf pro his comeuppance once and for all."

"My darling husband," said Patty, "I've never known sanity to shape hardly anything you've ever done as a pastor. But you know as well as I that the Bible reserves all vengeance for the Lord. Romans 12:19–21. Do we need to look it up, dear?"

"I'm not calling what I have in mind 'revenge.' It's a lot more nuanced and profound, Spirit-led even."

"I see. This doesn't have anything to do with the broken stained glass window, does it?"

"What makes you think that?"

"As my memory serves, Millicent Brandt phoned the parsonage in tears on the Monday evening after the Big Bertha Fundraiser and wanted to know exactly who would be replacing the shattered historic window 'given sacrificially and without fanfare' by her grandfather at the turn of the twentieth century. You hung up and called that blowhard LeBleu. Heated words, as I recall, including your veiled threat to withhold communion from the lanky Louisianan at the very altar rail where a shard of broken glass came to rest upon one of the needlepoint kneelers, piercing Myrtle Wilson's naked kneecap the following Sunday after she so graciously agreed to provide her backyard as a landing strip. I've never seen so much blood at a Lutheran celebration of Holy Communion. A clarification before we go any further. Who the hell is Bertha and what did she have to do with all that nonsense?"

Bill laughed for the last time that evening. "You've always had a sharp mind, my dear. It's been three years! You're good. You could have been a prosecutor in a court of law. But let's remember, please, that I'm not the one on trial here." With narrowed eyes, Bill smirked at his wife. "A Big Bertha is a golf club, a large driver. Rusty sells them out at the course and still thinks he can hit the damn thing farther than any human being in the history of golf, alive or dead."

"Ah. Maybe they should have called it a Big Bill. Well, you know the rest. Rusty left Good Shepherd with his inflated pride (and, presumably, the money raised by the property committee) and threatened to publish your rising golf handicap and other fabricated nonsense in the club newsletter if you ever pressed the matter. You happily hunt lost golf balls now and never see the man. Why not let it go?"

"I'd be glad to let it go, but I overheard that cocky bastard embarrassing a child the other day. Timothy needs a hidden defender; he's only nine. Jesus said something about going into your closet in secret to pray. Matthew 6:6. I know every inch of that course, much of it crawling on my belly, clandestinely. I can quote the Bible, too, you know."

"And so can the devil," said Patty. "Luke 4:9–11. Let's hope your lofty motives remain pure from such a rarefied height of judgment."

"I already told you I'd be on the ground."

"Slithering in the woods, right? Do I need to say more?"

*

Every summer before school resumed, Rusty LeBleu invited his twenty-five golf protégés to pull a number out of a hat. The boy who selected number seven received the high honor of playing head-to-head against the former All-American golfer at LSU (a claim never verified by anyone at Mountain Glen) in eighteen-hole match play, "a shootout between an Unforgettable Legend and his hopeful student," as it was annually billed in the local newspaper by an anonymous submitter.

Names of the lucky youth and the dates they'd been demolished by the club pro were etched on a copper plaque mounted on a large rock adjacent to the eighteenth green; a list of proud twelve-year olds who'd all, nonetheless, been utterly embarrassed by the end of the tenth hole. Rusty would unfailingly aim his putter at some imaginary bird on the horizon and say with a rub of the lad's head that bordered on a rough push, "Ten up with eight to play. Looks like that special number seven from the Bible wasn't so lucky for you after all, young man. You'll improve with time and perhaps try to take down the Rust-Man on some golden fairway in the future. Here's a wooden token for a free soda at the snack bar. Enjoy."

He'd invariably flick the token end-over-end at the boy and walk triumphantly to the clubhouse with a fawning group of sycophants in tow. A larger crowd than one might guess followed the proceedings, usually a gallery of old men who didn't have much else to do and the other twenty-four boys who didn't draw the magic number.

Bridget was in charge of the selection process that summer as eager boys gathered around the LSU cap, full of pieces of paper marked from one to twenty-five. To this day, she won't reveal how Timothy Robertson, a nine-year-old playing his first year of golf, managed to draw the seven. The match was set for the last Friday morning in August.

*

Forecast for Bridget's last week of summer employment before returning to school were blue skies and moderate temperatures, perfect weather for crowded tee times promising hefty tips that would chip away at expenses for the coming semester. Bridget was a little tired of the job and all the incessant flirty comments from men over three times her age, including the bloviated banter of Rusty LeBleu, who never seemed able to stop talking about his fabled golf prowess. She was glad to hear from Pastor Bill, especially when she learned it involved the collaborative and holy defense of young Timothy Robertson, the cherubic boy taken under her wing that summer like the little brother she'd never had.

"You need to remember," said Bridget on Thursday night before the match, "that Rusty doesn't allow cell phones for any of the cart girls while on the job. He thinks we'll talk too much. Pretty sassy for a man who literally can't stop talking, don't you think? Anyway, we need to think of another way to communicate."

"You know the tall grass at the edge of the ravine just below the seventh tee box?"

"Sure," said Bridget. "How could I forget? Where I leave you a beer on Monday afternoons, right?"

"Exactly. Miguel and Tomas call it 'Satan's Seacoast Hideaway' for reasons I've never completely understood."

Bridget laughed. "I love those guys. Maybe we're about to find out. Or, maybe we can help rename it when this is over. So, I leave messages at our beverage drop-off point in the ravine, right?"

"Yep. Right there. Bring a pen and some paper. I'll be there, hidden until the crowd passes, then cross over to the woods off the fourteenth fairway."

"Can't wait, Pastor Bill. You've taught me a lot over the years. Especially how God needs a little human help from time to time. Listen to this and then I'll hang up."

Bridget pulled a harmonica out of her shorts pocket, laid down the phone receiver, and played the first notes of "Amazing Grace."

Timothy Robertson rises early on the morning of the big match, steps out on the back porch to look for Venus, his favorite planet, promptly throws up over the railing, and phones his friend before sunrise to tell her, timidly, of his decision not to play.

"Look, I'm sure you're nervous," Bridget says. "I still get nervous at Clemson before a final exam or a date with a new guy. But listen, little brother, you can do this. All you need to do is finish and then your name will be forever etched on that copper plaque. Won't that be cool? And you're three years younger than most of them! You'll be famous—like that young kid in the Bible, Samuel, called by God to do something special. Remember that sermon Pastor Bill preached about that little boy? Well, probably not. You were only six at the time. Go drink some ginger ale and try to eat some toast. I'll meet you early at the course. I'm scheduled to drive the beverage cart around for the whole match. I'll be with you every step of the way. I promise."

At 9:00 AM on the first tee at Mountain Glen, Wally Benson, the aging octogenarian, former club champion, and erstwhile member of the property committee at Good Shepherd Lutheran, reads a prepared script (penned by an unknown contributor) into an ancient and crackling sound system, creating so much feedback that Myrtle Wilson—who'd forgiven Rusty for the unfortunate kneecap puncture-wound and was hanging on the golf pro's left arm for the opening festivities—loudly bellowed, "God-dam it, Wally, can you turn that blasted contraption down a notch or two?" Myrtle was constantly forgetful of her maladjusted hearing aid.

Most in the crowd laugh. Twenty-four young boys look at each other, grinning with raised eyebrows, as if they'd each just gotten away with something. Wally ignores Myrtle's instruction and booms into the microphone, "From Lafayette, Louisiana, pride of the Bayou, three-time All-American at LSU and one-time coach of Chi-Chi Rodriguez, who taught the little dancing spic everything he knows about this great game, I give you the man who needs no introduction, our own blue-eyed Rusty LeBleu!"

The gallery claps hard enough, but Wally also overlays the applause with a decades-old recorded crowd reaction lauding eventual winner Jack Nicklaus at the 1972 Doral Open, where Rusty had volunteer-caddied one spring break for Floyd McWherter who failed to make the cut by a wide margin.

Rusty doffs his purple and gold cap, bows several times, and twirls his Big Bertha driver like a magician mounting a stage. As the drive splits the opening fairway and reaches its apex on the way to a soft landing 335 yards away, Rusty shouts, "That one's for you, Myrtle!" The elderly saint, a Lutheran with Argentine descent, responds with a knee-buckling swoon as if Fernando Lamas has descended from heaven onto the first tee.

Timothy is so nervous he can barely grip the club handed to him by his mother, caddying for her son with a squeaky pull-cart in need of strategic lubrication. "And give it up, ladies and gentlemen," Wally booms from the script, "for the little fat boy from Fingerville, South Carolina, Timothy Robinson!"

Bridget glares at Wally from her beverage cart, later reporting to Bill that she couldn't decide which made her angrier, the derogatory diminutive or the error in announcing her young friend's last name, both jabs concocted by the snickering golfer high-fiving several of the boys as Timothy teed up, only a few noticing his tears.

"That vile asshole," she hisses through clenched teeth. Bridget retrieves her writing pad from the glove compartment of her beverage cart and writes Pastor Bill a short note.

*

A small man wearing a ski mask waits for the crowd to make its way down the number one fairway before he opens the car trunk, slings a pouch over his left shoulder, and furtively enters the woods. Bill wonders what his bishop might think of all this, but only for a moment. The pastor knows, deep in his heart, that he's on a mission of justice for the Lord Almighty.

Zigzagging down trails known only by fellow ball hunters, he takes his time reaching the ravine below the seventh tee box, occasionally looking rearward to insure no one is following. Bill enters the hideaway undetected. He has plenty of time to think and pray while lying on his back, looking through the branches of the rhododendron at the cloudless sky.

The beauty of match play is that an inferior golfer—perhaps dozens of strokes behind in a traditional round—can, with a little luck and (in this case) the Lord's blessing, remain competitive against a much better opponent. Timothy had an ugly twelve on the opening hole as Rusty scored a workmanlike par-four after missing a makeable putt, but the pro was still only one-up for the round.

Bill occasionally hears loud roars and deep groans from the approaching gallery. He fidgets a bit from his hiding place, trying to interpret the crowd reactions, but mostly waits with the honed and peaceful patience of a seasoned clergyman for the crowd to assemble on the tee above.

There were actually two notes left by Bridget in the sealed Pringle's canister hidden among the weeds at the bottom of the ravine. Bill waits for the entourage to pass before reaching out to retrieve them. The dear girl has also left him a cold beer, which he begins to slowly sip in the shadows.

The first note brings a smile. After six holes, Rusty is only two-up on their young friend. The rubber snake Bridget planted on the second hole between the club pro's six and seven irons in his LSU-engraved golf bag so unnerved the Louisianan—who'd been bitten as a child by a canebrake rattler in a woodpile on his grandfather's farm—that he conceded holes two and three while sipping sweet tea in the shade with his head in Myrtle Wilson's lap, as she fanned the local hero and hummed the Bayou Bengal fight song. Rusty recovered nicely to win holes four, five, and six.

"That Bridget," Bill thinks. "She knows the power of serpents from Scripture. The girl should become a pastor. Screw biology."

Her second note revealed the name and number of a certain golf ball. "Perfect," Bill says, a little too loudly, still grinning from the sound of 500 golf balls dropped from the sky and thumping near the tee during Rusty's interrupted backswing, resulting in a topped tee shot into the bowels of the dark ravine. The helicopter pilot, Bill's former parishioner, called Rusty the following Monday to apologize, insisting he was trying to make an air-drop at Leroy's Driving Range and Pool Hall Emporium across town. Bill quickly did the math in his head. He had 8,500 left; not such a large sacrifice.

The crowd descends into and through the ravine, almost to the seventh green, a hole he later learns was won, amazingly, by young Timothy. Bill drops the ball he just found into his handy pouch, but not before holding the shiny Titleist with a black number one up to the dim light filtering into his hiding place, the initials RL penned on the ball with a purple Sharpie. The pastor again pulls on the ski mask, emerges into the bright sunlight, and climbs quickly up the hill to his favorite shortcut, a five-minute walk to the thick woods along the fourteenth fairway.

*

When Bill was a seminarian and working summers at a camp called Lutherland, near Asheville, he received a note of reprimand one August, just prior to the beginning of his senior year, from the seminary in Columbia.

Dear William, the letter began. *It has come to my attention from the esteemed Director of our historic camp for fledgling Lutherans, nestled in our Lord's beautiful North Carolina mountains, that you and several summer chums—undoubtedly intoxicated with your own irreverence and perhaps gin spirits—recently devised a rather tawdry golfing amusement dubbed "Closest to the Cross," actually clubbing seven-irons across fabled Lake Lewdhorn from a crude tee box above the dam towards the very foot of the illumined source of our salvation. God will not be mocked, William. Rest assured that if this little game is ever repeated, your future at our seminary is tenuous. I understand your own tee shot clanged off the left extension once cradling our Savior's exalted elbow. An impressive shot to be sure, sir, but never to be duplicated in your lifetime. I shudder to contemplate the landing spots of your co-conspirators' tee balls. Get your act together, man. Sincerely, Rev. Dr. Luther T. Shealy, Acting Provost.*

The letter, much longer than the excerpt included here, stunned Bill in its hypocrisy (Jesus would've loved golf) and the blind eye turned towards much seamier incidents that summer at the camp swimming hole involving lewd and rather horny counselors, ironically befitting the lake's curious name. Further details from that summer will not be mentioned here, but the letter (still intact in Bill's pastoral file at synod headquarters, even in retirement!) underscores the need for measured propriety in describing subsequent developments that Friday morning with one Rusty LeBleu. Myriad pranks and ploys hatched by Bridget and her favorite pastor merit inclusion in this tale levying biblical humility upon a pompous braggart, but depiction of a single remaining plot twist seems prudent for those learning of this caper, perhaps decades hence, who may wittingly attempt to besmirch the reputation of a faithful servant of the Lord.

*

Rusty's tee shot on number fourteen uncharacteristically draws hard to the left and caroms off a tall oak tree into dense rough. Few can ever recall such a staggeringly impressive presence dropping his shoulder and causing anything resembling a duck hook. But this has been a surprising day all around. The local legend is somehow tied with a nine-year-old with only five holes to play, causing the gallery to swell with residents from the surrounding neighborhood, including at least seventy-five noisy children who've heard the news. Young Timothy Robertson has instantly become something of a local hero, win or lose.

Walking up the right side of the fairway, pausing to retch into a garbage can adjacent to the cart path, the young boy receives a cold Sprite from his female friend, a nice photo op for the local reporter capturing a scene and effectively diverting attention from the opposite rough where a masked man slithers in the tall grass.

It doesn't take long to accomplish the exchange. Bill quickly locates Rusty's tee shot, confirms the two initials, and replaces the sparkling Titleist with another bearing the number four. No one comes close to observing a man crawling back to the dense cover of the dark woods.

From the rough, Rusty impressively nails his second shot to within three feet of the cup and easily wins the hole. With momentum clearly in the rangy Louisianan's favor, he also wins fifteen and sixteen, closing out the match three up with two holes to play. "Better luck next time, Tubby Timmy. At least you get your name on the plaque."

On the fringe of the sixteenth green, surrounded by admirers including Myrtle Wilson, nearly overcome by the early afternoon sun, Rusty raises the winning golf ball as several cameras click to capture the moment. The staccato chant of "L-S-U, L-S-U" accompanies the golf pro as he heads towards the snack bar until a young woman, departing her parked golf cart, runs across the green and asks to see the ball.

*

Opie and Andy again walk to their favorite fishing hole as Pastor Bill turns down the volume, providing his own version of the familiar whistling while engaging in a little dance on the way to the kitchen for an evening snack.

"Let me get this straight," said Patty. "You basically cheated so Timothy could win, right? Now where in the Bible is there evidence to support that?"

"Look, the Israelites needed a little help in embarrassing old Pharaoh, right? I wouldn't call parting a sea cheating, but rather a manipulation of the playing field. That's all we did."

Patty rolled her eyes.

"And even Rusty had to concede that he played the wrong ball for three holes, clearly grounds for disqualification. Any so-called professional golfer should know that. I didn't make up the rules."

"Next you'll be comparing Timothy to young David who slayed the giant."

"The kid needed help. That's all I'm saying here. Hey, I forgot to tell you something."

Bill slipped into his tennis shoes, ran across the wet lawn to his outbuilding, and returned wearing the ball-hunting pouch.

"I see you haven't emptied it to add to the 9,000 others," said Patty.

"Actually 8,500, but yeah, you're not going to believe this." Bill carefully dumped the contents of the pouch onto the den carpet. "When Bridget asked to see the now-famous 'winning' golf ball, I simultaneously looked down in the woods at my feet."

Bill counted the balls again for Patty's benefit.

"Exactly as Rusty's face fell in shocked recognition, I found this one." Bill held the ball high in the air, a Callaway.

"My one-hundreth ball of the day. Now how about that? Maybe there's hope for the guy yet."

2.

God's Scorekeeper

Wrigley Field, Chicago
August 13, 1968
9:17 AM

DR. SAMUEL HORNSBY WAVES at a grounds keeper who is leaving the maintenance area under the left field stands to start his precise diagonal outfield mowing pattern, an old-school detail appreciated by many diehard fans who will begin arriving shortly after noon for the 1:30 PM first pitch with the league-leading Cardinals, now thirteen games ahead of the hometown Cubs in the National league standings, with roughly a month and a half left in the season.

Sam's head is filled with various numbers and obscure baseball statistics. He mounts the ladder above the center field bleachers that leads to a trapdoor allowing entrance to the old manual scoreboard installed by club president Bill Veeck (as in "wreck"), who also first planted the tenacious "Japanese Bittersweet" ivy (the name always reminds Sam of a former college girlfriend) that covers the expanse of the outfield wall. Sam recalls yesterday's game (a win) where Cardinal center fielder Curt Flood raised both arms—a local ground rule signaling to the umpire a ball lost in the famous foliage—as Ron Santo trotted into second with an easy double.

The wiry professor, nearing sixty-five, retired last December as homiletics instructor at the Lutheran seminary in Hyde Park and was almost immediately offered a part-time job by Cub manager Leo "The Lip" Durocher, whose infamous and boisterous mouth also announced itself with genealogical regularity in the Hornsby family. Sam and Leo are distant cousins and often meet for a post-game beer in The Pink Poodle—the private press lounge originated by team owner, P. K. Wrigley—to discuss baseball's seamier side, but also what Leo calls "da teeological beauty uh da game."

Even though Leo is rarely a churchgoer, he still appreciates the methodical and repetitive mystery of the Lutheran liturgy and knows of Sam's long affinity for numbers and order, which also often produces harnessed synchronicity in a player's approach to his job. "My Gahd, Mantle wears that lucky number seven. You can tell me more about the Bible's take on that, Sam, during the next beer. But what a mess the Mick has made of his crazy life."

The job seemed a perfect match for Sam after forty years of weary listening to young preachers whose neophyte oratorical skills were shaped (at least during the previous ten years) more by the country's social unrest than the Bible. Each morning, during his devotional time before perusing the box scores in *The Chicago Tribune*, Sam wondered if his hero Karl Barth (who would die in Switzerland four months later) lamented the rather lazy exegetical skills of modern preachers who had all but abandoned the Scriptures in their sermon preparation, favoring instead the latest screaming headline.

As Sam climbs the ladder to the scoreboard, the temperature is a comfortable sixty-eight degrees. The challenge for a man his age is not the climbing (repeated many times during a game on ladders within the multi-tiered interior), but rather the rising heat inside the board's arithmetical innards.

Sometimes it felt like Sam and his numerical cohorts were slowly basting in the late innings from the radiant heat. The predicted high for today's game, with a slight wind coming from the southwest (favorable for homers), is a manageable eighty-two for any so-called "bleacher bum." For Sam and his fast-moving cohorts inside the scoreboard, however, almost constantly in motion to hoist the five-pound steel panels into place, the temperature could easily reach one hundred and five.

The lanky Canadian, Ferguson Jenkins, the scheduled starter that afternoon, will undoubtedly feel the cooling winds of Lake Michigan between innings in the Cub dugout. The breeze, however, won't reach Sam Hornsby.

As the National Anthem rises around Wrigley, Sam pokes his head through a rectangular fifteen-and-one-half by twenty-inch opening in the scoreboard, looks out at the field and the fans, and remembers his faculty colleagues at the Hyde Park seminary campus. He also recalls the wild ride of the nation, particularly in the city of Chicago since John Kennedy's assassination, and the strongarm politics of Mayor Richard Daley as he forcefully attempted to quell all the unrest.

Dr. King's death, only four months before, still hangs like a pall over the stadium. Fans file in seeking a break from the daily news. Given work schedules, Sam often wondered *how* 35,000 Chicagoans regularly filled the Wrigley stands during the middle of the day, but he certainly understood *why* they came.

Always with hesitation, Sam's right hand covers his heart during the anthem as he feels the old pinch of loyalties between his country and his God. "There shall be no other gods before me," a commandment his pastor-father taught him as soon as the two-year-old could speak. Sam loved his country but often felt the old tension in competing allegiances.

The eye-catching 1966 *Time* magazine cover story asked the question, "Is God Dead?" The question was a rather misleading reference to a popular body of theological thought. Harvey Cox and his winsome colleagues were not so much referring to God's inability to shape and heal the world but rather to a secular society that rarely took time to explore the sacred writings where God's healing ways are revealed, rendering the deity dead by default. The formation of young pastors, understandably itching to hit the streets with a prophetic message, was an ongoing faculty challenge.

Sam still worries that many pastors graduate from seminary with an academic degree but no real spiritual depth; a lasting armor surely needed to stand up to the forces now tearing the country apart in a land where so many seem far from free. It's during thoughts like these that Sam always recalls his biblical namesake who long ago as a lad heard God's voice calling in the night. He hopes his tenure as a seminary professor was bolder than that of Samuel's mentor, Eli, who was enamored more with popular perception than with tradition and whose vacuous life eventually (and literally) collapsed under its own weight.

As the anthem concludes, Sam takes a seat on a metal folding chair. In the short lull before the first pitch, he double checks the sequence of a large stack of steel numbers and turns on the ticker tape machine that will spew forth updates of other games from around the nation, all noted with up-to-the-inning precision by a sweaty crew of three busy men.

As the Cubs take the field, Sam's focus completely leaves Hyde Park and his former life. His surname takes over, channeling his great-uncle, Rogers, whose career batting average of .358 is second only to the great Ty Cobb. The next two hours will be a mad scramble across catwalks and up and down ladders, the call of scores and the rattle of numbers intermingling like a measured poem.

Third Inning

The Cards jump on Jenkins early. The Cubs come to bat in the bottom half of the inning trailing by two; the deficit could've been easily more. A flustered Fergie throws down his glove in disgust in a corner of the dugout. Leo already has a reliever warming up in the bullpen.

Sometimes Sam and his crew can see fans in unusual attire through the narrow slats in the scoreboard, even though their gaze cannot rest upon much of anything for very long except the changing numbers. Today an old-timer arrives dressed like he's ready for a Bears game, sitting in the bleachers wearing a vintage 1935 coonskin coat that must be hotter than the interior of any scoreboard.

The men once saw a beautiful woman during a Pirates game who was escorted from her left field seat for sunbathing in the altogether. From a hole in the back of the scoreboard during an especially long lull for the seventh inning stretch during a Braves game in June, the crew saw a very drunk couple copulating on the rooftop porch across Waveland Avenue. The woman, leaning across the porch railing, seemed to offer an ecstatic bellow for the Cubs just as a partner mounted her from behind, but the supportive shrieks for her team were masked by the "L" train that rumbled by at the very same moment. The frenzied pace of the fast-moving numbers renders these comical glimpses rare.

Compounding the sweaty challenge of interior scorekeeping is working in reverse, backwards from Sam's point of view, so that the fans can read the box score. For Sam, fluent in the Hebrew and Aramaic languages (read right to left), the directional shift is less of a problem. Stan and Lou, his co-workers, require a bit more time to think.

Santo laces a double down the left field line to tie the score after three innings. The phone rings on the second tier of the scoreboard; it hardly ever rings unless the men have made a mistake. (Against the Dodgers last month, a "2" remained upside-down for three innings.)

It's Leo. "Sam, what the hey? I didn't think you guys had letters up there. It should be 3-3 after three, but goddammit there's a three-letter word spelled out instead of the bottom home team line."

The game is televised on WGN. Sam takes a quick look at the monitor mounted on the interior wall. Leo was right. Instead of 0-1-2, recording the runs for the Cubs in the first three innings, Sam saw the letters S-I-N.

Fourth through Sixth Innings

In the middle three innings neither team scored a run. Instead of goose eggs, brief couplings from the seven deadly sins appear in the visitor and home line after each team records their allotted three outs (no more than a minute for each word before vanishing). In the middle of the fourth, the word *lust* is spelled—with a full three seconds between each letter—as a topless Marilyn Monroe look-alike bolts onto the field from the stands, quickly apprehended by two grinning members of the grounds crew. At the conclusion of the same inning, in the home half of the line, the word *envy* methodically appears as the public-address system announces the day's prizewinning ticket holder: Gracie McFadden of Moline, Illinois, who wins an all-expense-paid trip for two for a week in Bermuda.

Leo again phones Sam, who'd already searched the entire interior of the scoreboard for contraband letter panels as the ticker tape piled up and other games across the country failed to receive prompt updates. "Sam, you're way too late for April Fools' Day! I know ya gotta wicked sense of humor under that serious professor mug, but let's save it for The Pink Poodle, whaddya say?"

Flummoxed, Sam could say nothing. The usually articulate professor is unable to utter words. Leo has already hung up anyway.

No player, visiting or Cubbie, has ever hit the Wrigley scoreboard with a home run swat, although Sam Snead used a four-iron from home plate in a 1951 publicity stunt that connected dead-center with an echoing clang in a nearly empty stadium.

At the end the sixth inning, however, bleacher bums begin pelting the center field scoreboard with everything from rotten vegetables (An aside: Who, dear reader, takes a rutabaga into a baseball game?) to glass beverage bottles. Sam phones for security after a ball peen hammer, skillfully aimed, whistles through a narrow opening in the aging steel structure and almost hits him in the head. The policeman on the other end of the phone laughs. "Ya' got it comin to ya, Doc!"

It's fair to say here, in defense of the fans, that the four words appearing in the fifth and six innings—*pride, anger, sloth,* and *greed*—were notably aggressive in their collective confrontation. The sixth inning required an exclamation point, bringing symmetry to the line score, since the revealed words only had five letters.

The bottom of that inning, curiously, turned each peanut vendor (about 150 men, all told) into raving versions of Saint John the Baptist, suddenly clad in camel's hair, a full beard, and a vending satchel laden with jars of honey rather than peanuts and Cracker Jacks. The 150 Johns simultaneously railed at the 35,198 fans about the dangers of greed with booming voices that didn't require megaphones.

The visuals for the other three words need not be mentioned here. Suffice it to say that Leo's next phone call is to Mr. Wrigley himself, who in turn calls the Illinois National Guard.

In spite of the stadium-wide mayhem, Ferguson Jenkins settles down and does not allow a run for the rest of the game.

Seventh Inning

Surprisingly, given the recent revelations, just the normal line score appears in both halves of the seventh. Santo's seventeenth homer of the season (a two-run shot to center on a 2–2 pitch from Ray Washburn) gives the Cubs a bit of breathing room. At the end of the inning, the hometown team leads, 5–3.

Jenkins continues to look solid, even stronger, as the game progresses. Notably, the fans are also calmer, perhaps wondering if their weekend diet of deep-dish Chicago pizza, famous throughout the Midwest, has been washed down with one too many beers, causing unwelcomed digestive hallucinations.

Sam Hornsby is also relieved. For the first time in his adult life, words (not to mention numbers) both fail and trouble him. He again searches the scoreboard's interior for errant vowels and consonants and can only unearth an old metal advertising sign of the "Doublemint Twins" (a fetching staple of the Wrigley chewing gum empire), posing as a pitcher-batter duo with attractive rumps held at impossible angles. "Double your pleasure, double your fun," the sign invites. Sam laughs at the irony of how his job has turned doubly challenging and is no longer pleasant or much fun.

During the lengthy seventh inning stretch, Sam considers, frantically, an old Bible story from the book of Daniel: the mysterious "handwriting on the wall." In chapter five of the book, in a scene from King Belshazzar's lavish royal ballroom, fingers of a human hand—appearing in mid-air without an attached body before a thousand guests—begin to write indecipherable phrases in large block letters along the main wall bordering the feast. No enchanter or local diviner can translate the meaning of the words; only Daniel, the young prophet.

The strange words include four, five, and six letters, respectively. (Sam notes the correspondence with the innings just concluded, slowly stroking his whiskered chin.) The words, written in Aramaic, announce judgment upon a king who failed to learn from the mistakes (and eventual insights) of his father. Daniel's honest speech cuts to the core: "You have praised the gods of silver and gold, of bronze, iron, wood, and stone, which do not see or hear or know; but the God in whose power is your very breath, and to whom belong all your ways, you have not honored."

Sam looks out over the crowd and starts to place a metal panel with the number two in the opening, still shaking his head to clear away the old story. He checks the ticker-tape machine as Jenkins runs out to the mound.

Eighth Inning

The word *gluttony* twice appears in the top and bottom half of the inning with its matching eight letters. For the first time during actual play, the word flashes repeatedly as Leo slowly ambles out to consult with his pitcher after Fergie allows two walks. (The manager had been planning to lose a little weight after the season's conclusion but thinks the added pounds actually extend the time the umpire will allow for this coaching consultation.)

In the bottom half of the inning, the reigning champion of the Coney Island Hot Dog Eating contest (weighing 350 pounds and flown in from New York, Sam later learns) parachutes into play with Ernie Banks at the plate.

Chicagoans may not enjoy graphic morality sermons, but they're not dumb. Soon after the rotund champion lands with a thump (amplified loudly over the PA system), disgusted and nauseated fans toss thousands of frankfurters onto the field and even soil the black uniform of the home plate umpire, Nick Mulvaney, with a long yellow mustard streak that will not easily yield to a stain remover in that evening's stadium laundry.

At this point, Sam's horror inside the scoreboard turns to laughter. The homiletics professor has never witnessed a more effective sermon. He fleetingly contemplates returning to the classroom but decides scorekeeping may afford more mind stimulation as he ages.

With order restored, the Cubs tack on five more runs. They lead, 10–3.

Ninth Inning

Jenkins pitches an uneventful ninth with fans heading to the exits on Clark and Addison Streets after the first out, a routine grounder to Don Kessinger at short. Sam (in a happy task long assigned to one of the score-keepers) will soon raise the blue flag with a white "W" so that passengers on the "L" train and nearby residents of the Wrigleyville neighborhood will know the game's outcome.

Held to only a single in four at-bats, first baseman Ernie Banks, Mr. Cub, now in his sixteenth Chicago season, stands before a television camera for a post-game interview. He removes his cap and offers his trademark smile.

"Well, that was just about the wildest game I've ever experienced here at The Friendly Confines," Ernie says. "Reminds me of a strange story from the Bible I learned in Sunday school as a kid in Dallas. Momma always wanted me to become a minister like my granddaddy, so I knew all of the Old Testament favorites. Today's game is oddly reminiscent of that strange handwriting tale from the book of Daniel. You know the one?"

The interviewer does not answer. A droning single-engine plane flies over the stadium, low enough to be heard, with a white banner trailing three initials and a single word: "MLK GRACE."

Ernie watches the plane disappear over the right field foul pole and again smiles. "I suspect Martin knows we still need a bit of that around here these days."

4:35 PM

The outfield bleachers are clear now. Sam is glad and has waited awhile on purpose. He climbs down the ladder leading from the trap door in the scoreboard and walks down the steps to where the center field seats almost reach the top of the ivy. Two seagulls call out to each other, heading towards Lake Michigan.

Sam looks down at the dirt warning track, out onto the historic field (empty except for the camera crew at home plate), and then turns, staring for a few minutes at the high scoreboard.

He again thinks of his faculty colleagues back in Hyde Park and also the pastoral graduates from the Class of 1967. "Scorekeeping," he admits to himself, "is a rather strange part-time job for a Lutheran professor in retirement." Sam reads the initials and word on the airplane banner as it passes over the scoreboard and wishes the plane had flown overhead a little earlier, maybe in the top of the ninth. "Always the issue of timing in preaching," he muses to himself.

Bob Gibson will be pitching tomorrow for the Cards. "Now that should be something to behold," Sam says out loud.

Sam waves at the grounds keepers, covering the outfield with a large tarp due to tonight's weather forecast, and hopes they fail to return his greeting only because their hands are full.

He walks along the left field foul line, avoiding the chalk, and past the Cub dugout, oddly on the third base side for the home team. He stands still awhile and takes in the sights and remaining sounds of the old ballpark.

Sam knows Leo will be waiting on him in The Pink Poodle with lots of questions he won't be able to answer. He's ready for a beer, maybe more than one.

3.

Impostor Pastor

FATHER BOB RISES EARLY to walk his dog, a black and white schnauzer, who sleeps nightly alongside the bed with a comforting snore, the fifty-year-old priest's faithful companion for the last eight Christmases.

When Bob wears his standard black clergy shirt around town with the white neck-tab insert, cleric and canine never fail to elicit smiles from the elderly women in his parish who always notice (usually from within the confines of their large automobiles) the comical color coordination between pet and owner. "Aren't they just adorably cute?" A comment which always irritates a man who, after six years of post-Bachelor of Arts education, tires of such inane words associated with his serious calling.

Bob cannot recall any stories in the Bible where Saint Peter and his companions were ever described as "cute." He almost said as much to Polly Lingerton recently on the sidewalk in front of the drug store after she patted Luther and then dared to pat him—on the head. Recalling the generosity of Polly's husband, a lead giver at Christ the King Catholic Church, Bob bit his lip until it almost bled.

Luther was a gift—on the ninth day of the season—from Bob's sister Cathy who believed in celebrating the ancient sanctity of the church year in all its fullness. The little schnauzer arrived under the parsonage Christmas tree with a bow and a name. Cathy thought both Bob and his church needed a little reforming.

*

At first glance that morning, nothing seemed to be missing from the parsonage. The back sliding glass door had obviously been jimmied by

26

someone who knew Bob and Luther's walking schedule, but not a single item in any room of the tidy home was out of place. Two police officers arrived and took fingerprints. The only match: the prints of the priest.

Bob had the door fixed by the church's property committee and thought nothing more about his suspicious guest intruder except to wonder why anyone might bother to break in. A pastor doesn't have a whole lot worth stealing.

Sometimes Bob questioned whether he should have used his academic talents in another field. During the long, isolated evenings at the parsonage, a variety of professions—especially those in which his early teachers predicted sure success—swam through his imagination. He traveled with Luther to distant locales for summer vacations and daydreamed about another life as an architect or espionage agent whose life with a woman named Ingrid began to take unsettling shape in his imagination.

Bob had prayerful confidence in God's call but occasionally wondered—even in the midst of the liturgy as he distributed the holy elements—if others sensed in him a siren tug to be somebody else. There was a movie he and Luther liked to watch together each Epiphany season about a man who suddenly disappeared from his small-town community, resurfacing in another country with a completely new identity. "I wonder if anyone would even miss me," Bob mused during the credits. A new life as a wise sage in another locale might be fascinating.

*

One day a stranger came by Bob's office with an unusual request. "I'll be honest with you," the man said. "I don't really believe in all these fantastic claims about Jesus being the Son of God. But I pretended to be a Catholic a couple times recently at worship services in downtown Richmond and really feel a special connection to your communion ritual. The bread and the wine seem to bring people together in a way I've never experienced. Could you teach me how to do just that bit? I'd be grateful and promise never to hoodwink people or use the holy meal strangely in some weird satanic ritual."

Bob looked at the man (who offered only his first name, Gary) for a while before answering—not with anger or annoyance, but with interest and a connection akin to recognition. There was something about Gary's eyes and manner of speech that suggested the two men had met years before. Bob couldn't quite put his finger on where.

"Well, I'm sorry," Bob replied, "but I can't do that. Actually, I'm not sorry at all. A priest studies and trains for years prior to ordination with master teachers and seasoned practitioners of the faith. There are multiple levels of understanding and centuries of theology behind the meaning and celebration of the Eucharist. I can't just show you how to preside at communion in ten minutes. To do so would be a colossal betrayal of my priestly vows."

"Aw come on, Father," said Gary. "It doesn't look all that hard to me. You buy a pack of pita at Ingle's and crack open a jug of Riunite and then pass it all around with a few holy words. What's to learn? I'd be helping people. Isn't that what Jesus said to do?"

The two men did not part that morning on angry terms; far from it. In fact, they laughed together upon saying goodbye after a chat that lasted almost an hour. Through his office window, Bob watched Gary exit the church building and cross the street. Even Gary's very slight hitch in his walking step, almost impossible to detect from a distance, reminded Bob of someone he knew.

*

Susie Baker works at Walmart across from the Little League baseball fields most weekday afternoons. Her relationship with Father Bob begins and ends at the checkout line although she finds him sort of cute (there's that word again) and wonders how any normal man gets through life without sex because the guys she's dated have all been as horny as field hounds.

Susie doesn't think much of Christians. She once told her sister, "A person could easily suffocate from what most people call 'Christian love.'" Susie left the church at age seventeen after her Pentecostal preacher conducted a devil-stomping one Sunday morning in order to "drive Beelzebub from the loose and lascivious loins of our teenagers." She's not entered a church building since but does like and admire Father Bob.

They sometimes chat for ten minutes or more across the conveyor belt on aisle eight late in the day when customer frenzy has died down. Luther is not allowed in Walmart so Bob's attentions are not diverted, focused solely on a woman who rarely receives uninterrupted listening from a man.

"I was sort of surprised to hear your car needed an oil change. My boss said he saw you in here last Thursday, and I could have sworn you told me you used Main Street Tire and Brake for all your automotive needs." Susie batted her eyes comically. "Was it our deep friendship, Father Bob, that caused you to jump ship? We appreciate your business."

Bob laughed and reddened. If truth were known, Susie could easily replace Ingrid as a foreign espionage agent's romantic companion. He sometimes allowed her kind face to enter his private moments of ecstasy in the parsonage bathroom, but never in Lent.

The priest prayed many times to be released from his lustful obsession and knew well its dangers from a full pastoral counseling load in the parish that ranged from common adultery to online porn addiction. The spirit is willing, however, but the flesh is weak. Even for a priest. What was the real harm in his little private indulgence?

"I'd been considering a change so that I could see my favorite checkout friend," Bob stammered, "but your boss must have seen someone else. I was out of town for a meeting last Thursday."

"Well, that's rather strange," Susie said. "My store manager just had that new laser eye surgery and can spot a shoplifter from a hundred yards. I'll ask him again, but he told me your look-alike was wearing a clerical collar and even answered to your name. Now wouldn't that be nice? Two men in town who aren't always on the prowl."

Bob gathered up his toiletry items, said goodbye, and outside took Luther's leash from one of his confirmation students who received three dollars for patiently occupying his dog. Bob and Luther walked home together, detained en route momentarily by Gladys Monroe, who rolled down her Buick window and called out how a cute little dog and his master matched so fetchingly.

*

In his first congregation after seminary in the southwest corner of Virginia, Father Bob received from a man named Slick (a Christmas tree farmer beloved by all) an old photograph taken in 1922, of a baptism in Helton Creek near Whitetop Mountain. Slick married into the Catholic faith as a young man but missed the emotion and close community of the mountain faithful with whom he grew up.

A young girl in the photo, a teenager, Essie, stands in the water up to her knees, arms folded below her chest. She's wearing a dress that extends below the stream's surface and she looks downward, pensive and a bit frightened, as mustachioed Pastor Blankenship (a Methodist) lifts one hand toward heaven; head raised, eyes closed. A cabin is in view in the background. Smoke rises from the chimney, a chilly day. The entire congregation—so many hats, suggesting a date near Easter—gathers on the opposite bank of the creek. Hands of support, just on the edge of the picture, seem to comfort and steady Essie. She's moments from going under. The assembled community seems to sense what's at stake in this old dousing into church membership. Many hands and hearts, with numerous acts of sacrificial love, have brought a new sister safely to this moment.

Bob looks at this photo often. Sometimes he recalls a story he once heard at a conference, told by a Catholic bishop who served a mountain parish in east Tennessee early in his career. An unbaptized man nearing ninety wanted to be immersed ("like it's supposed to be done") just after Easter in the cold headwaters of the river that ran below the church building. The novice priest reluctantly agreed. The old man made it through the first dunking but came up sputtering after the second and headed for the riverbank. "The Father and Son were hard enough!" the old man yelled. "I can't take the Holy Spirit!" The man's entry into the church historical register included an asterisk and the curious annotation, "partially baptized."

Remembering the story never fails to make Bob laugh, but mostly he looks at the photograph of Essie's baptism with tinges of dismay and regret, love for a church whose spiritual core is slipping away. He wonders if even three people from his parish might attend such a baptism today, the normal celebration of the sacrament occurring on Saturday mornings after a frantic and fearful mother has phoned the church office with the words, "Will you do my baby?"

Bob usually agrees, knowing he'll probably never see the mother or the child ever again; a sacred ritual reduced to magical fire insurance. More than anything he can consistently articulate, this skimming of the sacramental surface by those who ask for his pastoral assistance stirs in Bob a fear that he's just about as needed as any credentialed justice of the peace in the lives of people who want a dose of deity in their lives but nothing too demanding.

Last Wednesday morning on his walk with Luther, Bob encountered an aging and lovable ex-hippy named Daniel who called across the Piggly Wiggly parking lot. "So very good to see you! I've been meaning to call and ask if you might preside at my wedding this April. My fiancée and I are expert spelunkers and want to get married inside Mammoth Cave in Kentucky. Won't that be cool? You'll tie the knot for us, won't you, Rev? We'll be glad to make a contribution to your church."

Bob found it difficult to summarize the demands and discipline of the Christian life within the marriage covenant in five minutes' time on a sidewalk, finally telling Daniel that he could not perform a wedding unless the bride and groom were members of his church and agreed to several sessions of premarital counseling. "It makes no sense for a Christian pastor to officiate at a wedding apart from a community of faith that will help hold the couple accountable to radical marriage vows, offering encouragement, support, and love all along the marital journey."

Daniel started yelling, loud enough to catch the attention of shoppers in the parking lot. "Well, thanks Father Bob! This is exactly why I'll never become a member of any church. You people are all so judgmental and exclusive! Who'd want to be part of that?" Bob did have the temerity to inquire who exactly was excluding whom here, but Daniel had already walked away and didn't hear.

*

The phone rang at the church office one Tuesday afternoon. Father Bob immediately recognized the voice. "Listen, I'm working this afternoon and I swear there's a guy in the store who looks exactly like you, even talks like you. He could be your twin, only slightly shorter with a very slight limp. My friend Katie on aisle sixteen checked him out about an hour ago. He didn't buy much—a few groceries, some firewood, and a small canister of propane. Katie said it looked like he was going camping. I think you'd better get down here. The guy signed your name to a check from the church. Katie didn't even ask for an ID because she thought the guy was you. But she got suspicious about the supplies and knew you probably didn't like camping so much."

On the drive to Walmart, Bob considered the implications. A woman he admired doesn't see him as much of an outdoorsman. This bothered him even more than the bogus check-writer and the obvious vulnerability of the church's financial accounts. "Why do women often see priests as effeminate china dolls who dress up for God?" he wondered out loud.

There was that priest played by the affable Richard Chamberlain who had the scandalous dalliance with Rachel Ward in *The Thorn Birds,* but Bob worried that Susie Baker has already made up her mind about men like him. He intentionally left Luther at home, whimpering, and decided to wear a tight church softball T-shirt that showed off his developing biceps that have indeed swelled a bit since joining CrossFit, the local gym run by friendly Pentecostals, a generous Christmas gift from the same sister who graced him with Luther. Bob suspects Cathy noticed the need for additional reformation in his life.

Always a slow signal near the bank, the light finally turns green and Bob very nearly hits a man wearing a black clerical shirt running across three lanes of traffic with two policemen in fast pursuit. It's not every day in a small town that one sees law enforcement officers with guns chasing a local pastor into a back alley.

Children on bicycles stop to watch. A boy drops his chocolate ice cream cone on the hot pavement. Bob hears a young girl say his name while she gazes in the direction of the running man. A siren sounds. Traffic halts in both directions. Motorists exit their cars to gape at the spectacle.

The two policemen lead their handcuffed suspect back to a waiting squad car. They push his head down, guiding him into the back seat. The man is still wearing a clerical collar. Just as the car pulls away, Gary, the man who wanted to feed people with the body and blood of Christ, looks through the tinted window at Father Bob and smiles.

*

"Wanda at the bank told me she vacuumed cash through the drive-in express tube to your look-alike maybe half a dozen times over the course of three weeks before she got suspicious and pressed the silent alarm button. She told me the guy's toupee flew off during the chase across Main Street after the cops blocked his car."

Susie laughs and leans across the table to lightly touch Father Bob's left wrist. "Hasn't been that much excitement here since the strip club opened east of town and the Baptists faithfully picketed the place for the first year before giving up." Bob senses warmth from Susie's hand that feels like something more than friendship.

She takes a slow sip from her mug. "I'm wondering if you find this at all funny now that it's over? The guy looked a lot like you except for the fake hair. I guess you have enough clerical shirts in your closet that you'd hardly miss a couple, right? And Wanda told me those church checks were way out of sequence. Nobody would've missed them. Pretty clever of old Gary. He wouldn't have fooled me, though. That is, if he'd tried to check out on aisle eight."

Bob and Susie sit together in the local coffee shop, sharing a piece of pie, right next to the front window near the sidewalk. The priest couldn't care less if anyone walking by wonders why he's sitting in broad daylight, talking with a woman. Let them gossip. The phone company needs a little excitement these days.

That evening, Bob checks the sliding glass door at the parsonage out of habit and makes sure that Luther has food and water. He's lately been reading the sixteenth-century theology of Brother Martin Luther, the good Catholic monk turned reformer who shook the world with his writings about grace and vocation. Bob is especially drawn to the writings about the priesthood of all believers, the notion that ministry can happen in any job.

In his study, he looks again at the photograph of Essie's baptism in the waters of Helton Creek. The hands in the margin of the picture look different to the priest this time—supportive, yes, but more. Just before she goes under, the people who love Essie seem to be leading her in a new direction. Towards the church's primary ordination that matters even more to Bob this night than a priest's.

4.

Orthodox Orthodontics

THERE'S NOT A WHOLE lot one can say while reclining in a dental chair with hands and sharp instruments filling your mouth. Rendered impotent and still, the tongue rests safely out of harm's way. Responses are limited to grunts and maybe a carefully timed eye twitch of assent.

A patient did rise once in acrimonious defiance and stormed out of Dr. Gaffney Fretwell's office with a partially completed mouthful of hardware, still wearing the protective bib and eye goggles. He tore out of the parking lot with a loud screech that turned heads in the waiting room, leaving a long black mark across the outer end of the orthodontist's reserved automobile space. But these instances are rare. Guarding against future volcanic reactions from other testy tooth customers, however, Gaffney's pristine black Lexus now resides in a secure mini-garage on the back of the property, just large enough for two small cars.

Dr. Fretwell wonders sometimes why he left the ministry as a young pastor to enter dental school. Ten years into a successful adult orthodontics practice ("young patients are squirmy liability nightmares," advised a friend), the money has certainly proven to be the lucrative enticement Gaffney anticipated while daydreaming during church council meetings about a future where no one could offer an oafish opinion about his annual salary.

But his wife, Miranda, has another explanation.

"Gaff, honey, you just couldn't stomach all the negative preachin' feedback. You went to seminary, and Joe the plumber thinks he knows as much about the book of Philippians as you do."

When Miranda starts with such explanations, the orthodontist's mind always rests upon a certain verse in chapter two from Paul's old letter to the good people of Philippi: "Let the same mind be in you that was in Christ Jesus."

Gaffney smiles confidently, comforted that he and Jesus are still on the same page. Though no longer identified by his clerical collar at work, he has retained a single black pastor's shirt, long-sleeved, which he wears to bed on special evenings when the children are away to lend an intriguing holy flair to zesty romantic dalliances with Miranda. She's had to sew the row of buttons back on the shirt numerous times after rambunctious romps around the house, fueled with a bottle of their favorite Merlot.

"But I think the final straw," she continued, "was the day when that loudmouth, Brenda Lowenstein, told you at the door after church that Saint Paul's thorn in the flesh was probably his closet homosexuality. You said 'enough of this horseshit' (forgive me, Lord) and applied at Johns Hopkins." Gaffney always laughed when his wife told this story at cocktail parties of the Upstate (SC) Malocclusion Association.

He still missed preaching, though, and realized early in his new vocation that a captive audience of one might be a bit easier on his nerves than trying to shepherd a parish of cats whose theological opinions were as varied as the colors of their twitching tails. Most patients did not mind Dr. Fretwell's dental homilies. He was a bit cheaper, they reasoned, than the competition across town. What could it hurt to hear a little Leviticus while having your teeth straightened? Gaffney was just offering a bit of wisdom on the straight and narrow to help pass the time.

And certainly no one could accuse the good doctor of false advertising. "Orthodox Orthodontics" was boldly emblazoned on his publicity materials. Even though some patients just assumed Gaffney had Greek ancestry, given the accent on orthodoxy, the business motto should have cleared up any confusion: "*God's Truth for Your Tooth.*"

*

Tooth manipulation is a painstakingly delicate art, but much easier than the straightening of souls. It's one thing to convince a patient to wear a retainer with regularity, but another endeavor entirely to coax a parishioner towards wearing the Word on a daily basis like the spiritual armor God intended. The Lord retains the right to allow his wayward children to experience the consequences of non-compliance. So does Gaffney, but he's still able to cash the checks of those who ignore his dental advice.

It didn't take long for Gaffney to discover that he could straighten teeth and preach at the same time. The word *misalignment* kept jumping off the pages of his dental school textbooks. "What is sin," he excitedly shared with Miranda after a long day in the library, "if not a misaligned act? Just as sin literally 'misses the mark,' a gummed-up life, so too with the sad reality of maloccluded teeth that damage the gums of God's children!"

From that day forward, Gaffney never attended an orthodontics class without his Bible. Like a premier athlete who suddenly realizes he can play two sports, he began to imagine a new business model that might catapult him to dental stardom among his peers, fighting tooth and nail to buck the odds—the nails, of course, from the very cross of Christ.

*

Dr. Fretwell always prepares the examination room with the help of his lovely assistant, Melissa, who has the annoying but endearing habit of saying, "Roger that, Ghost Rider," to just about any dental instruction Gaffney might offer. With his receding hairline, Gaffney does indeed favor an older Nicolas Cage but Melissa does not bear even a faint resemblance to Eva Mendes. The cryptic reference to the movie largely confuses patients.

Gaffney quickly describes the various tools and probes he'll be using, laid out in neat metallic symmetry at eye level of the reclined. The four nails are always placed last in the line of objects and never initially described by the doctor who always waits patiently for the mildly sedated to ask.

"Oh, these?" Gaffney asks, offering mock surprise at their presence. "Driven into his hands and feet, these are the four nails of Jesus Christ, who suffered on the cross so that we might not have to suffer if we only trust in his name. I hope this thought brings you comfort and alleviates your suffering in life just as we will relieve your physical suffering as we bring your misaligned teeth into proper relationship. You do trust me, don't you?"

No one ever asks if the nails are authentic or duplicates.

"Melissa, can you hand me that first probe?"

"Roger that, Ghost Rider."

The evening before he was to start the process of installing braces for Bruce Tidsworth, a new patient, the boys (ages eleven, nine, and seven) were out of town visiting their grandparents in Charleston, "The Holy City," a name which pleased Gaffney and his beautiful wife.

Enjoying her time alone, Miranda decided to open a bottle of Merlot. She'd bought a case on sale at Trader Joe's, where, remarkably, they could be purchased for only three dollars a bottle. She sensed that her husband's week had been not only long but also hard. Miranda blushed, despite being alone, and then chuckled to herself when the words *long* and *hard* called to mind goals for her private leisure time with Gaffney later that night.

Miranda had planned the evening with exacting care and wifely love: his favorite meal of Carolina pork barbecue with a tangy mustard sauce, accompanied by collard greens and candlelight; a negligee (freshly laundered on the gentle-spin cycle) that still held its dark leafy-green vibrancy after years of romantic use, eliciting many fond memories of their rock-solid marriage; and a hint of very expensive perfume Gaffney had purchased for her one summer in New York City while engaged in continuing orthodontic education concerning the fascinating correlation between sleep apnea and gum disease.

Waiting for Gaffney's arrival home after his last patient, Miranda thanked God in a quick prayer that her children and her marriage were "absolutely and biblically *normal*, Lord Jesus, and not like these other portable freak shows we have to look at every day on the sidewalks of our great country." Her concluding "Amen" was timed with Gaffney's Lexus turning into the long driveway paralleling their exquisitely manicured lawn. "Juan and Carlos do outstanding work for people of Mexican descent," Miranda once confided to her garden club.

The evening was perfect except for two small details that possibly shaped the next morning's dental encounter with Mr. Tidsworth. After a lingering hello-kiss in the living room entryway, Gaffney noticed a purple stain, circular and somewhat moist, on the Fretwell family Bible, passed down from his great-grandfather, a Baptist preacher well-known across the state of South Carolina.

The Fretwells had made their peace with wine consumption early in their marriage, convinced that Jesus' impressive miracle at Cana strongly suggested the Savior supped at some point during all the wedding merriment. "The matrimonial venue must have seemed like a noisy winery after Jesus did his thing!" Gaffney once thundered during an old sermon.

But the wine stain on the family Bible was a bit more than Gaffney could bear, especially since he'd warned Miranda many times about using the Word of God as a common coaster. Standing in the spacious alcove of their home, he was torn between anger, tears, and genuine disappointment in his wife. "We are forgivers in the Fretwell family and I forgive you, Miranda, but that stain on the cover of Papa's King James Version will be hard to forget." His words hung like a cloud over the perfectly prepared barbecue.

Miranda had seen Gaffney's anger many times, especially during their days in the parish as he dealt with wayward church members. And he was a man who cried easily (accentuating his attractive virile masculinity) when the moment called for tears. Jesus not only drank wine; he also wept. Miranda was proud that her husband's emotions mirrored the complex feelings of her Lord.

It was Gaffney's disappointment in her that felt like a knife-stab to the heart. She vowed to make the rest of the evening as memorable as possible. And if she needed to act like Delilah (or even Jezebel) to make her husband recall why he married her, then so be it. What she had in mind would erase any lingering wine stain sullying the Word of God. If her plan worked, she'd only need to wink in the alcove in the days to come to steer her husband's imagination in a preferred direction.

In the bathroom that night, after the dishes were cleared and left in the sink ("It's the least we can do for Alejandra," their faithful morning maid), Miranda's mind wandered to the pages of Song of Solomon, by far the raciest and most sensual section of the entire Bible. Gaffney confessed to her once that he'd read it as a boy with a flashlight under the sheets after saying good night to his parents.

Chapter seven lingers over the female lover's thighs, navel, neck, and nose. Miranda wasn't so sure about the comparison of breasts with "twin fawns of a gazelle" as hers lacked any spots, but she was careful to apply perfume to all requisite body parts, in accordance with the sense (and scent) of Holy Scripture. These loving ministrations would make her favorite orthodontist forget all about the silly stain.

A repentant wife walked into the bedroom's candlelight glow. She looked lovely, biblically prepared for her waiting husband. The couple smiled at each other across the room, privately giving thanks for their many blessings compared to the trials and tribulations of other couples sadly residing outside of the Lord's grace and guidance.

Perhaps Miranda would have missed her had the three glasses of Merlot been dialed back to two. But as the beautiful wife of nearly twenty years took a step towards the eager orthodontist, her right foot pinned to the floor the fluffy tail of the Fretwell's family feline, Precious, whose scream could have easily awakened the dead.

*

At first, reclining in the dental chair the following morning, Bruce Tidsworth could not figure out how Dr. Fretwell knew so much about him.

Bruce had been warned by a friend about the dental instrument sequence and immediately noticed the four nails at the end of the row. An Episcopalian, Bruce was prepared for the little sermon and actually didn't mind a bit of Bible coupled with the installation of his new braces, even though he'd heard the scriptural interpretations at Orthodox Orthodontics could border on conservative-sketchy.

He even enjoyed Melissa's constant references to a movie he detested. It did seem rather odd that she would refer to an ex-preacher wielding sharp dental instruments as a "Ghost Rider," especially since the Apostles' Creed was pretty clear that Jesus' resurrection was bodily. The risen Savior was no ghost after his release from the tomb.

A seminary professor of Gaffney's had told his introductory hermeneutics class that one of the reasons Jesus refused to embrace Mary Magdalene at the tomb was that the Lord was naked, his folded graveclothes leaving him nothing to wear but a gardener's hat. "Jesus had a body at Easter, my young preachers, and Mary noticed!" But Gaffney wrote the old coot off as a horny widower who read his sordid imagination into way too many biblical texts.

Just for fun, Bruce considered trolling his orthodontist by asking how a King James Version-toting Christian reconciled his faith with the existence of ghosts, but the period for patient questions had passed.

What bothered Bruce a bit, as the doctor began to reflect upon the nail wounds of Christ, was how Gaffney Fretwell somehow knew he was married to another man. Bruce and Mark had only recently moved to South Carolina. They'd been together twenty-five years last April and celebrated their anniversary by getting married in New York.

Then Bruce remembered. His medical records had been forwarded by his previous dentist who always made a habit of including in file notes personal information ranging from hobbies to family relationships, in order to become more personally involved in the lives of her many patients in a very large practice. There were several notes about Mark and his employment and hobbies in Bruce's file.

This would explain why Gaffney now said, "And one of the most egregious and festering modern wounds in the body of our Lord, his church, must surely be the sin of homosexuality. A nail wound—an abomination according to Leviticus 18—that must especially bring great pain and consternation to the communion of saints. Wouldn't you agree, Mister Bruce Tidsworth?"

Each of the five syllables was enunciated slowly, with unusual emphasis on the hard consonants, as the doctor glared at Bruce over his mask while holding a narrow dental mirror (resembling an extended index finger) that gleamed in rays of the morning sun now slicing through the window blinds.

"It's unnatural, isn't it?" Dr. Fretwell inquired.

"Roger that, Ghost Rider," chirped Melissa.

The mild sedative given to Bruce prior to the procedure now caused him to smile, which seemed to anger the orthodontist. Bruce could not be sure, but he told Mark later that afternoon that he could swear Dr. Fretwell said, "God did not intend for us to put certain things in our mouths. Now did he, Mr. Tidsworth?"

Mark laughed at Bruce's hazy recollection and said, "Yeah, come to think of it I can't remember a single time in the Bible where any of God's people got their teeth straightened with braces. I guess Gaffney may have to put his orthodontics money where his mouth is."

*

Miranda was a bit worried about her husband. She understood perfectly how Precious's howling kitty-cat scream temporarily ruined the mood. But even the green flyaway babydoll, her go-to garment, had not awakened the desire of a weary dentist as she'd predicted. Miranda felt like flying away to her mother in Charleston and crying on her shoulder. The wine stain must have been a bigger deal to Gaffney than she'd judged.

Now there seemed to be a lingering stain hanging over a marriage she once thought was made in heaven.

Gaffney taught their Archway Young Adult Class the following Sunday at First Baptist and gave a short personal testimony—after an exposition of the first chapter from the book of Romans and Saint Paul's condemnation of "men committing shameless acts with men"—concerning the sanctity of keeping the marriage bed undefiled according to the clear guidance in Hebrews 13. Gaffney glanced at Miranda lovingly as he spoke. Perhaps everything was okay after all and the young orthodontist was simply overworked.

Miranda recalled a Bible verse from Proverbs about wifely patience and drove to the local "For Your Eyes Only" adult superstore to purchase a new negligee, this time fire engine red.

*

In many ways, Bruce was the perfect orthodontics patient. He kept a spare box of rubber bands handy in case he ran out on Sunday when the local drug store was closed. He rinsed dutifully with the special mouthwash and was careful in the first weeks of his realignment to avoid certain foods that might jar his new hardware.

"I'll never kid you again about not brushing as a child," Mark said one evening.

Bruce (on the advice of his Episcopal priest who confirmed him in high school) was a daily observer of several classic spiritual disciplines. "You're as relentless with your oral and spiritual hygiene," Mark joked, "as Gaffney is with his torrent of disconnected Bible verses. It dawns on me that you're concerned about getting straightened from the inside-out and good old Dr. Fretwell frets about hammering people straight with his 'truth' from the outside-in. Didn't Jesus have something to say about that?"

The waiting room was empty when Bruce returned to Orthodox Orthodontics for his three-week checkup. He'd taken a late afternoon appointment so that he and Mark could pick up an elderly neighbor, Rose Jenkins, who'd been discharged from the hospital at noon that day after a severe bout of vertigo. Rose could be a little nosy, but she meant well. "I don't care what you boys do behind closed doors, but I do know you're two of the nicest neighbors I've ever had. You're like sons to me. Please don't ever move."

Bruce reclined in the normal position upon entering the examination room. He'd just heard low laughter and whispering through the thin drywall of the adjacent bathroom.

"So how are we today, Mister Bruce?"

Bruce made a mental note for his patient evaluation form, on his desk at home, to include a suggestion that Dr. Fretwell (and all doctors, come to think of it) should refrain whenever possible from using the "royal plural." Surely, Bruce thought, he wasn't the only patient who found this irritating.

Gaffney seemed especially animated, more than called for even on a Friday afternoon. And Melissa, breaking orthodontic office protocol in a bright green miniskirt, appeared even peppier than usual, sprinkling her "Roger thats" with an Irish brogue that just seemed wrong to the reclining dental patient, even though Saint Patrick's Day fell on the following Monday, making for a long weekend for the office staff who would all observe the holiday. Bruce had seen the notice on the sliding-glass checkout window in the waiting room.

"Everything looks great!" exclaimed Gaffney. "You've done an outstanding job, impressive in your attention to detail. Any questions?"

Bruce was almost disappointed. He'd been bracing himself for various scriptural daggers from Deuteronomy and even forgot to mention a historical peculiarity he'd discovered concerning the surprising sexuality of one King James, who commissioned the famous 1611 English translation of the Bible, Gaffney's favorite, albeit wine-stained.

Bruce got the sense of being rushed out the door. He descended the porch stairs to the parking lot and heard the front door-lock resoundingly click. The illuminated roadside sign of Orthodox Orthodontics went dark.

*

Because their sons were away that Friday evening for a mission trip with Bible Boys, an exciting new ministry at their congregation, Miranda decided to open a chilled bottle of Chardonnay and slip into her new vivid red clothing purchase.

It was a warm evening for mid-March, so she took her glass and the wine bottle onto their protected and enclosed back porch where the young couple had made love, scripturally blessed, under "God's starry canopy" (see Psalm 8) several memorable times. The air felt good against her skin as the cat purred at her feet and rubbed against a bare calf. Miranda decided to leave Precious outside that night upon Gaffney's arrival home. He'd told her he'd be a little late due to the long holiday weekend.

Miranda heard the high cackle of a pileated woodpecker in the woods behind the backyard fence as dusk fell on the quiet neighborhood. She poured a second glass of wine and prayed for their close church friends, Todd and Barbie, whose college-age son, Andrew, just told his parents he had a boyfriend at Clemson.

"And Lord," Miranda prayed, "I know you hear the laughter of those who mock pure Christian lives offered in obedience to your holy Word. Just as you thwart the mocking advances of the woodpecker with the solid boughs of the mighty oak, raise up all your children like trees beside the living water, leading them to place their peckers in God-ordained and righteous places."

Miranda knew her words were tinged with the warm glow of Chardonnay, but she felt good, blessed, about her little family as she entered the kitchen and pulled the sliding glass door against the chill of the evening air. She looked at the clock. 8 PM, a little later than Gaffney had predicted. "That poor man," she said out loud. "He must be working overtime on somebody's misaligned mouth."

*

At first, Bruce panicked that afternoon upon feeling his back pocket to pay for a few groceries in the Express Checkout at Ingle's, but he quickly realized he'd left his wallet on the counter in Dr. Fretwell's examination room.

His heart sank when he saw the empty parking lot at Orthodox Orthodontics, especially since it looked like he'd be without a driver's license until Tuesday morning. Bruce drove to the back of the property and admired the cute mini-garage, but discovered no cars. Mark would kid him all weekend about his forgetfulness and probably also pinch him several times for neglecting to wear green.

Bruce exited his car to think for a few moments. They'd indeed moved to a beautiful part of South Carolina. Purple crocus was in abundance in the yard next door. Yellow forsythia bushes were in bloom along the length of the property border. A pair of wrens had started a small nest in the azalea branches next to the building's brick wall. "What an amazing world God has created," Bruce thought. "Including absent-minded knuckleheads like me."

On a whim, he tried the back door. The doorknob gave way to Bruce's quick turn.

Would walking through an open door be regarded as breaking and entering? As he crept down the hallway leading to the examining room—listening to the melody line of "Nearer My God to Thee" over the soft office Muzak still playing well after closing time—Bruce doubted that the mission to retrieve his own wallet would qualify for attempted burglary. There it was on the counter, just below a row of key hooks.

*

Mark listened, enraptured, later that evening as the two men shared their own bottle of wine, an unusually smooth red called "The Black Dog" from a Virginia winery that had made its debut at Ingle's only last month. The friendly checkout person, Susie, had stashed the grocery items at her feet near the cash register until Bruce could return to retrieve them.

"Oh, you're gonna love this new vintage," Susie said. "My girlfriend and I took several bottles to Myrtle Beach a few weekends ago and went into the waves after midnight. Even in March!"

Loud laughter in a building that was supposed to be empty had prompted Bruce's intrepid investigation at Orthodox Orthodontics a few hours earlier. "After collecting my wallet, I heard a laugh as haunting as a hyena's from around the corner and down the long corridor. And you know me, I had to investigate."

Mark briefly rolled his eyes. "I followed the laughter and peeked into the room. Nobody heard me. There in the other examining room at the end of the hall was Gaffney Fretwell, reclining in the patient's chair and wearing only a pair of green satin boxer shorts. Above him stood Melissa—you know, the annoying 'Roger that' girl I told you about?—sporting a rather provocative leprechaun outfit that covered very little and left even less to anyone's imagination, including mine. I watched them for awhile. Who could turn away? It soon became obvious that they'd both dipped into the nitrous oxide and were high as kites. Hell, I even started laughing softly a bit at the spectacle."

Mark was giddy as he asked, "Did they quote any Bible verses to one another?"

"You're a wicked man," Bruce replied.

"What else did you see? Tell me more."

"I decided it was time to get out of there. I tiptoed back down the hall and even pushed the car across the parking lot a little way before starting it. You know me, the silent type. I did take a little something before leaving. Do you think God will forgive me?"

Bruce raised something small and metallic towards the light of the sofa lamp. Mark read the name "Lexus" out loud and laughed.

*

The phone never rang Saturday mornings. Especially intriguing was the illuminated caller ID: "Gaffney Fretwell, DDS." Bruce allowed the call to go to voice mail.

The voice was lower in volume than usual. "Look Bruce, no games. It's uh, Gaffney, your orthodontist. I know you were there at the office late yesterday, right? I noticed your wallet was gone. It, um, had to be you. And even though you took the car key (yes?), I want to thank you for saving my marriage. I was about to do something even more stupid than you no doubt saw. I heard a car leaving the parking lot and went to investigate. I know I've said this already, but that was you, right? Had to be you. Your clandestine visit must have been authored by God Almighty because it woke me up, my friend. Really jolted me awake."

Bruce shook Mark's shoulder at the word *awake* and held the phone to his partner's ear as they listened from the beginning.

"And so, I had a lot of explaining to do with Miranda, especially after being dropped off at the house after dark with no car. But I confessed everything. And I'm sure that you, of all people, know how confession is good for the soul. We'll be okay. Hey look, I want you and your friend to come to our twentieth-anniversary service where we renew our wedding vows. It's at First Baptist next month on the fifteenth at three. You don't have to let me know or anything. Just come. I owe you a lot. I hope to see you there."

Bruce erased the message. He looked at Mark for a long time, shook his head in wonderment, and rose from the bed to make scrambled eggs for breakfast.

*

The minister at First Baptist had unusually large hands that completely covered Gaffney and Miranda's laced fingers. His voice boomed over the crowded sanctuary. "And Jesus also said that 'everyone who looks at a woman with lust has already committed adultery with her in his heart!'"

Even from the church balcony, Bruce could detect a slight reddening in Gaffney's face that undoubtedly had more to do with his inner thoughts than the unusually warm April day. Mark leaned over and whispered, "At least we're kosher concerning one clear warning from the Sermon on the Mount."

Lengthy prayers for the attractive couple followed. Their boys were dressed in tiny matching tuxedos and stood behind their parents in descending height. The service concluded with a thunderous admonition to all gathered.

"Those whom God has joined together let no man put asunder!"

"And no woman either," whispered Mark.

Gaffney hugged both men at the reception, just after they signed the guest book. Bruce dropped a car key in Gaffney's left coat pocket.

"I'm so glad you're here," said the glowing orthodontist. "Bruce, you saved my life. I owe you. Take home some of those little finger sandwiches, okay? I know you people like those dainty white bread pastries and we'll never eat them all."

As Mark and Bruce drove home from First Baptist that afternoon, they talked about their move to South Carolina and how things were changing.

"Just look at that, for instance," said Mark.

As they drove past Gaffney's office, both men laughed so hard that they had to pull off the road.

The word "Orthodox" had been removed from the illuminated sign.

"Roger that," said Bruce.

5.

Black Dome

WHEN BIG TOM WILSON finally found my body, I'd been dead almost eleven days, face down in a pool at the base of a twenty-five-foot waterfall that now embarrassingly bears my name. There's an irony here, of course, as I actually died in the waters of my baptism years before in New England, when Abner and Phoebe, my loving parents, handed their squirming son to a Connecticut pastor who proceeded to drown me in the name of the triune God per the rather stark theological claims found in the sixth chapter of the book of Romans.

Given this preeminent spiritual death, you might accurately say I'd only stopped breathing when Big Tom, the famous Carolina mountain tracker, found me prone and stone cold in the chilly headwaters of Sugar Cane Creek. (Forgive me, I probably don't need to include this little-known detail here, but the man's moniker actually described the girth of his groin area more than his linear height. I'm a scientist, after all, and measuring things has become my obsessive specialty.)

The newspaper report says I apparently "slipped at the top of the falls in the falling darkness" (clever yet distracting wordplay), striking my forehead on an impressive protrusion of granitic gneiss bedrock (my professional assessment, not the cub reporter's) on the way down, surfacing a bruise as black as these old mountains. A cranial blow rendered an unconscious state that led to the subsequent drowning. A pocket watch quickly malfunctioned with the drenching. Considerable overblown interest swirls around the frozen hands stopping at precisely 8:19 PM (four seconds shy of 8:20!) on the evening of June 27, 1857, a Saturday, but I'll get to all that directly. The report claims I was lost. Not a chance of that, dear reader.

The first burial occurred down the mountain in Asheville but my pliable and portable bones now reside at the foot of an observation tower at 6,684 feet, the highest point east of the mighty Mississippi, where every Tom, Dick, and Harriet with a camera now take vacation Polaroids after hardly breaking a sweat during the short climb from the parking lot. I actually overheard one portly man say he'd had five breakfast lattes at the nearby state park restaurant. He seemed rather proud of this culinary extravagance, loudly passed gas, and headed back down to the gift shop.

They dug me up with the careful and exacting precision inquisitive young children might exhibit in extracting rubies from the roadside tourist mines southwest of here near Franklin. "Let the dead bury their own dead" said Jesus, so I suppose my old misguided colleagues in the geology department at the University of North Carolina were twice-mortified in their obsession with my remains. The second interment was surely a well-intentioned accolade lovingly offered by friends in Chapel Hill, but the showiness seems like an indecent avalanche of attention for a Presbyterian minister, don't you think?

To measure the elevation of the massive Black Dome, I did repeatedly bust my hindquarters, so to speak, while crawling through a confounding maze of laurel thickets with my fragile barometric instruments, disturbing enough yellow jackets in the process to rival a biblical plague. But these rather modest efforts hardly merit the surname Mitchell assuming permanent (blasphemous?) affixation to such a magnificent invention of the one and holy God.

The Yancey County coroner officially declared the drowning an accident. Please pardon any scolding judgment here, but what a maroon.

*

My parents named me for the renowned prophetic protégé from the book of Second Kings and while I do admit to occasional and flamboyant broadsides from both pulpit and podium, no verbal venom ever approached the intensity leveled at those forty-two boys by the crusty man of God who called down ravenous tooth and claw from two fabled she-bears for the rather innocent impertinence of laughing at the prophet's shiny pate, as luminously bald as the Roan Highlands. I had most of my shaggy mane at the time of my death, as (unflattering) photos will attest. The hairline was receding, I'll admit, but so should any concerns you may have about my temperament.

I can be touchy about my trusty measuring process with those who attempt to challenge my findings, but espouse Saint Paul's wise instruction, originally intended for the church in Ephesus, to never allow the sun to set upon one's anger. My seven children sometimes tested me, and I gently slapped one of them after worship one Sunday for escaping Maria's lap and crawling under the pews to the front of the church, interrupting my sermon. But I felt so bad about striking little Charles that I woke him up later that night and offered my heartfelt apology.

I do envy Elisha's prodigious telepathic skills used artfully and diplomatically to thwart, for example, the Dothan night raid orchestrated by those pesky Arameans and sensed early on that one of my students, Thomas Clingman, seemed to challenge just about everything I said during his geologic matriculation at Chapel Hill. It didn't take a rocket scientist (wrong century, yes, but I'm a savvy ghost) to detect the young lad had me squarely in his budding professional sights. Tom was an exceptionally bright lad who became a state senator and eventually a general in the Confederate Army, but you'll discover I'm not the only rival who thought he might be heading over the edge. The historical record will show that he spent time in an asylum with the insane. No more about that residency will be stated here, but I trust you'll keep the alarming tidbit in mind as this dark tale unfolds.

*

I've never trusted Frenchmen, but it's hard to overlook the impressive volume of work by Andre Michaux, known as the Versailles Vagabond by those who admire him. (I just concocted that nickname, to be honest; never entirely trust a Shade.) Andre roamed these mountains several decades prior to my own traipsing and was probably the first white man to visit the range of peaks he dubbed The Blacks. Michaux, an exceptional botanist, knew his flowers, but I humbly take great pride (if that pairing is possible) in proving that my mountain (forgive me) exceeded in height his false assertion that Grandfather Mountain near Boone seemed the tallest in all of eastern North America.

Science cannot seriously entertain words like "seemed." Precision and accuracy are demanded by those who laud veracity as among the most noble of human strivings. Barometric pressure does not delude. The

French—I understand completely from my early pursuit of Maria—adore the rhapsodic and romantic. Mountains have this effect on many. But for obvious reasons, few scientists write poetry. Data determines authenticity.

So, in a one-horse wagon, I set out for Morganton with a full array of measuring devices and a dozen seminal books from my (not to brag) 1,900-volume home library—a rackety week's journey from Chapel Hill. Friends who accompanied me remained several days in the small mountain town to file barometric readings at a known elevation. We then compared those readings to others I faithfully recorded at precisely the same moment astride the Black Dome. The ascent, even with a guide, was arduous.

Some laughed at the enterprise, but using the differential in the barometer data at the two locales and a rather complicated mathematical formula, I indeed determined that Andre was passé. University faculty members were thrilled with my discovery. Southern journalists, agog with excitement, filled countless columns with obvious pride when, just before the Civil War, there was not much to brag about. One reporter falsely embellished my supposed encounter with an angry mother bear, printing a picture of a nasty leg gash actually inflicted from a broken and razor-sharp rhododendron branch that sliced through old trousers on the way up the mountain. For the most part, however, newspapers recorded a rather heady time based upon my accurate measurements and multiply-tested facts.

Nationally, a plethora of colleagues came forth with acclamation and praise. All, in fact, save one.

*

The towhee sounding down yonder Balsam Trail reminds me how much I once enjoyed sipping a certain English tea at sunset. These mountains are especially breathtaking at dusk. The red spruce forest that once covered the summits of various peaks in these Blacks has been severely decimated by acidic air pollution drifting eastward from the unchecked industry of the Ohio and Tennessee Valleys. My favorite tree, the eastern hemlock, under which I spent many lovely nights, has fallen victim to that infernal imported pest, the woolly adelgid.

But as shadows lengthen and night obscures the serpentine parkway winding along the spine of the lower ridge in the distance, I still find myself in awe of the stunning beauty revealed from this lofty vantage point. I regret the volume of heated words exchanged about something as relatively mundane as elevation. Does it matter to God, ultimately, which mountain in eastern North America is highest? I know it mattered to me, but perhaps what Christians need centrally in this harried and pompous land is learning to love silence. "Let anyone with ears to hear listen," said one far wiser than I.

Beginning in 1855, a two-year war of words in state newspapers commenced with my former student who'd by then become a North Carolina congressman. I use the word "commenced" in rather jocular confession as the controversy over the East's highest peak had been simmering between us for quite some time. I'm not usually an aggressive man. There was that time I called Ravenscroft, the recalcitrant Episcopal bishop, a horse's ass for insisting that tradition and all his high church frou-frou should be allowed in theological debate alongside the authority of scripture. He even accused me of bringing a "too Presbyterian" influence to my young charges at the university. The compelling facts of Scripture should suffice. Jesus never wore one of those silly miter hats, now did he?

My question to any sane person (forgive me; broken promise via innuendo) is simply this. Why would a barometric plebe trained as a cunning lawyer so vehemently challenge the measured findings of a man of science? There can be no logical explanation to such a query. Professional jealousy? Academic recognition? Even higher political aspirations? An unbalanced cognitive inheritance? (Oops, again.) I'll never understand Clingman's obsessive elevation challenges in a million years, if the Lord grants me that many trips around the sun on this mountain before bringing his servant to the promised celestial home where these annoying personality peccadilloes (*peccare*, to sin) are truly no more.

The ill-fated journey back to the mountain that June was decidedly unwise in retrospect. No one believed his wild assertions save a few sycophants in Raleigh. But there was something about his challenge that gnawed at me. Maybe I *had* made a mistake or two. The last barometric reading was recorded in dense fog. I'm a fallible man. Even Maria, my love, will tell you as much. I set out in spite of her sad and downcast demeanor. She'd been patient with these western junkets in search of a new elevation frontier, but there are emotional limits even for saintly spouses.

I won't deny that the thunderstorm did complicate things. The trail became horribly muddy with maddening rivulets of water obscuring the way. In places, it was hard to take another step without slipping. I became disoriented at times, but never lost. The mountain's familiarity was like the back of my hand. The later newspaper reports are simply erroneous in suggesting I was adrift in the forest during bad weather.

It did seem wise to abandon the trail (one could hardly call it a path at that point), descend into the middle of Sugar Cane Creek, and make my way off the mountain until the storm passed. Though wet and slick, the rocks provided much surer footing than the mud. Following the creek downstream would eventually lead back to my starting point. I could begin another ascent of the mountain the following day.

Lightning and thunder cracked and boomed all around, shaking the surrounding trees with violent intensity. I occasionally saw flashes of color behind me and at one point heard branches snapping, attributing the sound to the wind.

Even in the driving rain, the waterfall, nowhere described on any existing topography map, was beautiful and mesmerizing. I took a long slow drink of the liquid at my feet and then the landscape beyond. Surveying the best route down and ahead from the top of the falls, I heard something unusual that sounded like a large animal emerging from the woods. From behind my left shoulder, Thomas Clingman jumped into the streambed, momentarily losing his balance atop an adjacent rock. Scratched and bleeding, he looked like he'd just seen a ghost.

*

At my tomb on the mountain's summit is a beautiful and appropriately succinct inscription: "In the Hope of a Blessed Resurrection." I'm rapturously filled with such marvelous expectation, but this in-between existence also leaves one so regularly restless, wandering around the woods wishing someone other than the Lord knew the truth of my demise. It's a small matter, I suppose. We all expire eventually. Any simpleton can measure mortality's incessant march.

But the rather sloppy accumulation of forensic evidence around the base of the waterfall still troubles me. The investigative blindness suggests I'm some amateur backwoods hack who possessed the compass skills of an addled Boy Scout. Please do not misunderstand. Big Tom receives full exoneration for his noble efforts. He was only asked to find me. And that the lovably oafish man did with courage and valor. But I still roam these highlands because no one bothered to closely examine the damn watch.

The watch discovered in my right pocket is not mine. Do you think a scientist of my stature would risk using some knockoff imitation dime store time-measuring device that would cease functioning upon submersion? Wake up, Sheriff Dullard! Just this single piece of glaring evidence would lead any intelligent investigator to surmise the presence of another human in the vicinity. And, Great Jehovah, such an observation would surely lead to a host of other possibilities.

For the record, I did not slip.

I was pushed.

And robbed.

*

Envy takes on a monstrous and sinister shadow even among men who are normally righteous and just. Perhaps that is why Pope Gregory, towards the end of the sixth century, was quick to include this foul four-letter descent into the dark side of covetousness among his now-famous compendium of the seven deadly slip-ups. (I trust the man's theological conclusions even though he too, at times, sported one of the daft and pompous hats, flirting with pride. Review your own list, sir.)

Poor Thomas wanted to discredit my elevation findings, to be sure, but I often wonder if he desired the fetching timepiece even more intensely. It was indeed a beauty, a close waterproof cousin to the original that debuted in London at the 1851 Great Exhibition. Whenever he was in my company, perhaps using the elevation controversy as a smokescreen, Thomas's eyes flitted to and fro like the small gold and silver fish that swam around the original Pettit pocket watch suspended in a glass globe filled with water in the grand exhibition hall. But, I digress.

I should have just given him the blasted toy. That would have allowed this restless geologist, pushing sixty-four when pushed, even more time to chronicle the intricate mysteries of the Black Dome, certainly avoiding the rather ironic black knot that came to adorn my own cranial dome, the ugly indentation still visible on this hardheaded skull.

Please pardon me. I just overheard. A park ranger is once again getting the facts of my demise all wrong.

Yet another tourist requires gentle informational correction through subtle means I'll have to quietly devise.

6.

Pastor Polar

5:07 AM. I'VE JUST completed my weight lifting routine in the garage (early these summer days to beat the heat) with an eighty-pound bar and precisely 115 bench repetitions in descending clusters of twenty, fifteen, and ten. That's 9,200 pounds, every other morning.

Now a battery of stretches on the living room floor including a yoga pose known as "the horse," involving opposite arm and leg extremities, balancing on one knee. Our cat, Portia, sometimes joins me. It's amusing to observe how her front and back paws extend to mimic my own stretch—a cat doing the horse.

Water bubbles in an early boil on the stove. Conserving energy, I turn off the eye. Upon stepping out of the shower the egg will be ready for me to peel. I detest wasting time. Several things can usually be accomplished at once with a little forethought. People could get so much more done in a day if they only stopped to plan and ponder. Sadly, most wait for the day to come to them. I know exactly what I'm going to do today at three and also at seven and for most of the intervening and subsequent minutes.

There's always a better way to accomplish the tasks we face. I've never understood why my declaration of the obvious annoys people. I tease my wife and children and tell them I can "see the future," but any high school graduate should be able to control most of the day just by using their God-given senses and adhering to what I call "Consequence Theology," the unfailing maxim that certain consequences always follow certain behaviors in a repeating pattern as obvious and expected as gravity.

My parishioners misbehave in creative and salacious diversity. I listen patiently to their errant exploits, nod caringly, but privately wonder: "Do you not recall what happened in Eden with punishment following prohibition as night follows day?" They often seem surprised to find themselves in sticky moral predicaments. Please.

*

6:14 AM. In my open palm rests a small oblong pink capsule, prescribed for ingestion thrice daily. I stop taking these periodically as they seem to inhibit social and creative alacrity, but my wife always threatens to leave me. She says I'm a mess without medicine, swinging between mania and lethargy and back again like a child on a swing set pendulum, but slower. Or maybe faster.

I'm told my perception of my state of mind is not reliable. I wrote a book once in ten days during a manic episode. I thought it was brilliant, but one sassy editor returned the manuscript with a note: "You'll need to change some of the grandiose claims in almost every chapter to have a chance for publication, not to mention any sort of viable readership." I replied with my own terse message that's best not mentioned here.

I tend to fluctuate between hiding my bi-polarity and crowing about it with the wrong people. Nothing to be ashamed of. (Or everything to be ashamed of, take your pick.) My great-aunt was lobotomized, suffering from schizophrenia, back in the dark days when science only knew lithium to be a light metal on the periodic table (#3 just after helium, which reminds me of a funny story involving balloons that I'll perhaps share later).

Aunt Sophie was whisked away at age twenty to a sanitarium just west of Little Rock and never mentioned again in family conversations until my livid mother discovered her name while sifting through an attic file cabinet the spring after my grandfather died. Mom confronted her dad's sister, another aunt. They drove to Little Rock the following July to visit Sophie, whose mind was gone and days were filled with drool and delirium. Although an Australian psychiatrist discovered the mood-leveling wonder of lithium in 1947, it was not approved for use in the United States until 1970, too late for poor Sophie.

Okay, so I did go a little overboard with my lithium advocacy that Sunday morning during the children's sermon, when I took my morning dose with a healthy glass of water right in front of the little tykes; the congregation observing, agog. I was trying to make a point about that poor Gerasene demoniac who bolted naked from a cemetery where he'd been chained, afflicted with what was surely some form of unnamed mental illness. "If he'd only had this little pill that I'm now taking!" their pastor thundered.

Coupled with the demise of the drowned pigs, it was just too many mixed metaphors for the boys and girls to digest all at once. I told them that lithium is a key ingredient in creating the color red in summer fireworks shows and compared the blazing night sky to what we all might experience in future celestial realms. They still looked at me with rather confused expressions. Even diminutive and brilliant Lilly, the church's resident prescient five-year-old whose answers I could always count upon, appeared befuddled.

I found it rather ironic that Susie Sanders called me a "swine" on the way out the narthex door and never returned to church. *Her loss.* I did receive an uncomfortable visit from the bishop the next morning that resulted in a signed agreement (really?) pledging to dial back my open endorsement of a drug as innocuous as table salt. Jesus said, "The truth shall make you free." The truth also emasculates ecclesiastical control freaks.

*

8:25 AM. I was just about to head out the door for the church office to interview a new secretary (we've had a series of resignations lately for reasons I do not fully understand) when an overwhelming fecal cramp sent me limping to the toilet. I always think of Martin Luther when taking a poop. (An odd phrase, don't you think? Shouldn't we be "leaving" such things?) The man was excrementally entranced. Here's a quote from the great theologian in this regard, offered from his deathbed: "The world is a giant anus. I am a large piece of crap. And we are about to rid ourselves of one another." Splendid analogy! There's the scatological departure lingo I'm craving!

I was thinking about this the other day. Have you ever considered how human shit (barring an enema-cleansing, but don't get me started) travels around with its owner all through any given day? While watering your garden, it's present with you. While jogging; up hills and down. Bicycling; mere inches from the saddle. During the ecstasies of making love (yes, even then). Any activity you might imagine includes this malodorous oddity being formed inside a dark cavity of stench and enzymatic gurgling. It's a sobering thought. A helpful reminder of our common mortality, don't you think?

I broached this fecal profundity in a sermon during Lent several months ago and, curiously, I haven't seen the McDingleberry family since. Of course, I'd never mention this conundrum during the Christmas or Easter seasons for obvious reasons even though the manger, please note, was not filled with sweet-smelling hay and the man (fully human!) had to go to the bathroom somewhere while trapped in the tomb for three entire days. So, give me a frickin' break, McDingleberries.

*

11:09 AM. The interview did not go well, at least from her perspective. She'd Googled a news account several years old (I had to admire her sleuthing abilities) describing my loquacious address to the assembled shareholders of Bethlehem Steel, oddly meeting (for Pennsylvanians) south of the Mason-Dixon in Atlanta for their 1976 annual review of company operations during the country's bicentennial. I inherited a bit of stock from the same grandfather who turned his back on Sophie and had every right to be present.

The reporter creatively described my address as a "biblical filibuster" resulting in my handcuffing and removal by local law enforcement authorities. That diminutive Asian doctor dragged from the overbooked airline flight looked like a cooperative candy-man compared to my ferocious verbal assault (resembling the prophet Amos) levied upon the wealthy elite whose negligent labor practices in the sweat shops of their sordid organization brought shame to the name associated with our Lord's birthplace. I suppose it didn't help that I was draped in the American flag and wearing nothing else.

The secretarial candidate wanted to know more about this old story from the infancy of my pastoral career and dared to ask if my temper ever flared in a similar fashion here in the church office.

So, I slapped her.

It wasn't a hard slap, but that rather aggressive facial caress essentially ended the interview. I would've never asked the woman about her weight (trust me, a fatty) and could not understand why she felt the need to get so personal about my past. Let me leave it at that. There's a policeman knocking at my office door and I need to see what in the hell he wants.

*

2:56 PM. I came across an interesting magazine article while waiting for processing in the county detention center. The essay was about Japanese beetles and their mating habits. My wife and I detest these little creatures that almost destroyed our crape myrtles last summer. We sprayed and put out traps; an all-out war on these ubiquitous vermin. Nothing worked. I peered into one of the traps and became intoxicated by a roiling insect orgy. Trust me on this: Japanese beetles are hardly monogamous.

I only raise the issue of monogamy because it seems rather odd of God to expect lifelong sexual fidelity from his human creatures when the insect world is fucking away like crazy with impunity, "Consequence Theology" be damned. What I've come to call the "insect exemption" has done little to deflect the accumulated ire of a confused family who never quite understood my serial relationships with Tanya, Vicki, and Natasha in three successive parishes where we had to depart rather quickly, under the cover of darkness, with no opportunity to offer even a sad goodbye to my faithful and adoring flock.

God "whistles for fly and bee" in the book of Isaiah. (Look it up, chapter seven). But do I ever get busted for whistling at and noticing women! Maybe I'll come back as a Japanese beetle in the next life.

*

4:04 PM. Coincidences occur so often in my life that they cease to astound me. I've stopped calling them that. The officer asking about the secretarial candidate's blatant lies happens to be a second cousin of the policeman who arrested me in Atlanta in 1976. Small world? Hardly. I've concluded that God leads anyone paying attention to a multitude of connections and intersections; so many, in fact, that any idiot must eventually conclude the "coincidences" are indeed authored by the divine.

Even beyond the genealogical gem we unearthed, I alertly noticed that the officer had a business card on his desk from a local company servicing HVAC units and this led naturally to a conversation about our common obsession in trapping cool air on early summer mornings with windows open (in order to lower the temperature in the house) and then closing them around 9:00 AM to stave off the air conditioning unit kicking on prematurely from the hellish South Carolina heat.

Are you following me here? They call me the "Air Trapper Controller" in my family and laugh mockingly at the many noble efforts to save a little money. I told my children the other day that people who refuse to trap air resemble those who see cash on their front lawns each morning and refuse to bend down and pick it up.

That got a laugh from the officer, but then the bastard had to turn serious on me. Secretary Fatso is pressing charges because she claims my light admonishment of her rude foray into my past left a small bruise on her already puffy cheek (if you get my drift) that I'm convinced was the quick work of some bogus makeup artist sporting a homemade window sign in a ratty downtown storefront.

*

7:07 PM. Well, I'm only a little late for tonight's church council meeting and suspect they'll forgive me for such a slight tardiness. However, I strongly doubt they'll overlook the mug shot in tomorrow morning's paper. I've developed an unusual sixth sense about these delicate matters. Even though I look rather dashing in the photo, the leaders of the congregation will undoubtedly express displeasure. These people *pose* as Lutherans by name, but know nothing of radical grace and often behave like common Pharisees.

This reminds me of the time I was leading a church council retreat at Sandy Run Lutheran Retreat Center and had just offered a winning conflation of heretofore disconnected thoughts on Queen Esther, the wee man Zacchaeus, and Nathan the prophet. My point was crystal-clear: that small people like me could rise to positions resembling royalty and speak winsome truth to the powerful. When Harry—a spry octogenarian elder who'd been baptized at First Lutheran as a baby—rose to challenge my biblical conclusions, patently obvious to any kindergartner, I confess to responding rather curtly with the word "bullshit."

His large ears with tufts of untrimmed hair and lobes as billowy as bedsheets were apparently offended by a word I then confidently claimed was in the salty vocabulary arsenal of our Lord Jesus Christ. (There is no Gospel evidence for this surety, but come on. The man who in most sappy Sunday school paintings looks like he just stepped out of the shower with a Clairol makeover coupled with an innocuously understanding gaze, a ridiculous piece of kitsch, instead must have possessed a rather sharp tongue that eventually got him killed with its sometimes-venomous aim. Just saying.)

So, I guess if the oafish crew of so-called church leaders still holds against me the use of an occasional profane expletive surely uttered by our Savior, they'll understand a righteous defense that my jailing prior to posting bond earlier this afternoon also coincided with the very hour and day that Jesus was falsely arrested.

*

2:43 AM. My wife thinks she has it hard just because the moving van fee she carefully researched online minutes before midnight seems to exhaust the little nest egg she inherited last fall from her deceased (and rather haughty) father. Well, cry me a river, woman. No one ever stops and inquires how I feel.

So what if yesterday happened to be her birthday? Does anyone care about my trying trip around the sun?

Okay, so I forgot about the party the kids had thrown for their mom. Miss Smarty-Pants had the audacity to tell me it was "only the latest episode in your long history of self-absorption." Not helpful. But I've forgiven her, even though it's difficult sometimes with her many personality peculiarities to faithfully enact Jesus' gospel admonition of seventy times seven. She's almost exhausted the limit there.

She loves me. I know she does. And the children, God bless them. They left me a slice of cake and a chilled tumbler of milk in the den, reminding me of all those years I dressed as the benevolent Saint Nicholas who cheerfully did so much for so many, especially the impoverished.

I'll tell you about that in a minute but first I want you to hear what my voice sounds like upon inhaling helium. (#2 on the periodic chart, as you recall, almost kissing the blessed element I forgot to ingest today.) The three balloons in the corner are surely meant for me, the children recalling with fondness the many times I've whimsically entertained them.

My voice on helium sounds very funny. Sort of like the cackle of a Maine loon.

You'll laugh.

I promise.

7.

Twelve Across, Twenty-One Down

THE PATH DOWN TO the dock is faint now, obscured with many summers of disuse by chokeberry bushes and stinging nettle, more accurately by the dwindling camper enrollment that finally closed this place about ten years ago. The eight-bunk cabin on the last ridge could badly use a new roof, but I doubt anyone cares much these days whether the structure slowly becomes part of the surrounding woods. Small pine tree branches are starting to poke holes through the rotting screens.

I ducked inside the door for a moment and could still hear the voices of adolescent males as they bedded down for the night. In fitful dreams, perhaps they tried to forget some of the stigma of Down syndrome, but I always envied the total lack of pretense with their bodies upon stepping out of the shower and such effortless ease with laughter, recalling the many ways I constructed some false façade to try to impress people (usually girls) who eventually saw through it all anyway.

There was this boy named Stan in one of my cabins. We called ourselves "The Fried Pies" and won a prize that summer for the most creative cabin sign. He went missing once when we traveled into the nearby college campus for lunch at the student union, a weekly trip by bus wildly anticipated by the entire camp. I couldn't find him anywhere in the dining hall and finally heard his loud giveaway laugh six serving lines away from our group. He was sitting with a table of college kids, a baseball cap with the university logo pulled way down in disguise. Stan resisted going back with me. Just for the moment, he was a real student.

I push on in the last hour of afternoon light down each descending turn in the trail, occasionally cutting across a switchback to save a little time, but could probably walk this path blindfolded in the dark. We swam at the lake every day, a welcome respite from upstate South Carolina heat. I break the stem off some trailside jewelweed and apply the soothing juice to a nettle sting—odd that both plants often grow together in the mountains, like some horticultural parable from the Bible concerning the proximity of good and evil.

Arcing sheets of rain in the distance move steadily towards the lake basin. My wife, Nancy, rolls her eyes when I mention my mysterious pastoral powers of seeing the future. This prediction, however, is rather easy. I'll be wet in fifteen minutes and regret leaving the anorak back at the car.

Nearing retirement after over three decades in the ministry, I know the climb out of here will be harder than it once was. I'm supposed to be watching my heart rate after coronary stent surgery last October, but it will feel good to be winded and out of breath, maybe a distraction after returning to a place I've been avoiding for the last thirty-five years.

*

In late summer of 1979, I was driving a fifteen-passenger van to pick up a group of female campers and their counselors on a remote peninsula that extends out from the dike road near the dam that created the lake, not far from where the Savannah River begins at the confluence of two other rivers on the state line. Jimmy Carter was in the middle of a tumultuous four-year term. Billy Joel sang on the van cassette tape player. I joined him for "Only the Good Die Young."

This was part of my job as camp director—scheduling, logistics, song leader, enforcer of the rules, and sometimes "lifter of spirits" when staff morale was low. It was a step up with more pay than another camp in North Carolina where I'd worked the previous three summers, solely as a counselor. This new job involved night residency with campers and all the challenges that could occur after dark, but less direct camper responsibility during the day.

I recall hating to fill out the counselor evaluation forms at the end of the summer for the camp owner who was known to give overly honest references (when merited) with future employers who called about past job performance. Many of our counselors went on to teach special education in public schools throughout the state. Listing employment at a camp of our stature looked pretty good on a resume.

Working with mentally challenged people attracts a rather odd as-sortment of personalities (including mine, I'll admit). Our staff that sum-mer was creative, funny, and rather warped. I had to confront a counselor named Mike who peed into half of a watermelon one night after the camp-ers went to bed. He did it for the shock effect on a weary staff and wouldn't have let anyone actually eat the thing, but still. Another pair of counselors, Joy and Trish, clandestinely arranged the camp's large and well-worn stash of flexible stuffed animals in a fascinating array of sex positions from the *Kama Sutra*. We found the little creatures in various poses of pleasure at breakfast one morning. This, too, required a write-up, but I included an asterisk for creativity.

The swimming site where I picked up the group was several miles from the camp. We had access to miles of shoreline with the van and a cantankerous pontoon boat that only worked about half the time. It was not unusual for me to pick up (or sometimes rescue) a variety of groups. This group was especially challenging for the six female counselors (college stu-dents from around the southeast) and included a camper whose potential seizures had to be monitored closely around water. She could say only three words: "Yep" and "Oh shit." The limited vocabulary became a running gag with most of the female staff, largely as a release to stay sane through a long summer. Another camper in this group, who loved the cartoon character Charlie Brown, said "penis" when she was trying to say "Peanuts."

As the van crept closer to the pick-up point, I noticed that all six coun-selors were linked arm in arm across the width of the road. Even closer, squinting, I realized they were all topless: twelve bare breasts in a row. I'd never seen more than two. Laughing, I got out of the van. We all knew each other pretty well. "*What* are you guys doing?"

Julie, the ringleader, was a junior at Clemson. "Well, we knew you were heading off to seminary this fall and plan to be married next summer, so we thought we'd give you this little dual gift from the six of us." Hard to find fault with that. We all piled into the van, campers and counselors wet from the lake. Three didn't bother to put their bikini tops back on until we reached camp. I can't recall laughing so hard, finding it difficult to keep eyes on the road ahead and not check the rearview mirror with a frequency that might seem weird.

The morning after Julie and I made out until 3:00 AM, twining slippery bodies in the lake's darkness near the dock (a large breach of professional decorum for a camp director, not to mention a future seminarian), I had to run from a 350-pound camper, surprisingly quick, who chased me around the base of the fire tower at the site of our Thursday Breakfast in the Woods. He'd poured more sugar into his bowl than Cheerios and was furious that I'd confiscated his source. His breathless southern twang still rings in my head: "*You just ought not take a person's sugar!*"

That's not all I should have never taken that summer.

*

An older colleague told me that pastors are among the last generalists, and I think that's about right. You need to know a little about a lot of things—theology, counseling, adolescent psychology, long-range planning, stages of grief, dynamics of trauma, Bible teaching, community organizing, spiritual direction, preaching, marketing—but not a lot about anything in particular. Add in the expectation of home and hospital visitation and funerals that occur like drumbeats in our aging congregation. It's always a full week with lots of unexpected changes in direction.

And horrible things happen. People come to my office in trust and, in tears, pour out the most amazing and agonizing things. I carry around a lot that never gets announced on Sunday mornings. Even Nancy knows only a fraction of what actually occurs in my work. Thirty years as a pastor has taken a toll, not only on my marriage.

My work has also served as a convenient diversion from the complicated geography of my own inner life. When you're trying to help others over the long haul, the cumulative ministerial mask works quite well in pushing down any darkness in one's own past, elevating at times a perceived false righteousness. I've had my fill of that—not only because it's simply a sham to try and live that way, but the lie I'd been carrying around for so many years was about to eat me alive. It's an old story, one that stretches back to Eden and the garden's first occupants who deflected guilt by trying to blame another.

The rain, a light sprinkle at first, arrives just about the time I reach the dock, the old floating site of many a swan dive and belly flop, still in surprisingly solid shape after years of neglect, the diving board long gone. I take off my boots, sit, and run my hand over the holes from the board's foundational bolts. A couple of discarded worm containers, lightly faded from the sun, suggest recent fishing here by local kids. The surface of the lake receives the first drops from low clouds and bream rise inches from my submerged toes, looking for food.

I've been faithful my whole marriage and recognize my need to say that to you (or maybe God) is probably still part of my denial concerning any responsibility in the birth of Julie Shebah's baby. Thirty-five years later, I'm hardly able to admit that the child was probably also mine. The inner geography is complicated terrain indeed.

It's raining harder now. Wet anyway, I strip off clothes and dive into the cool water, swimming deep to touch ancient river stones at the bottom, releasing the oxygen in my lungs to stay down longer. Jonah spent three dark days in the belly of the great fish. Wishing for more time than that, the last air bubbles rise towards the surface and I finally push off the bottom towards a murky light.

*

Julie wrote me late the next fall after camp concluded. I'd stayed a week longer than everyone else to finish reports, clean and stow gear, and service the pontoon boot for winter storage. I was deep into New Testament Greek one afternoon at the seminary library when old Dr. Fritz (crotchety master of the card catalog and also the campus postmaster) handed me a letter at my study carrel with handwriting I at once recognized. "Looks like you have a fan club," he growled.

Julie and I remained friends the morning after the memorable "Twelve Across" encounter at the lake but, as summer flings go, never really talked more about whatever we'd briefly shared. The last days of the summer sped by. We exchanged pleasantries when passing during the week and even sat together at the staff send-off, assuming (at least I did) that we'd probably never see each other again, moving on to separate lives. Julie told me once she didn't believe in God. My work and hers as a school teacher in another state didn't offer much chance for future intersection.

I read the letter once, and before leaving the library, a fifth time. There was an old incinerator on the west side of campus. Returning to my apartment that afternoon I dropped the letter in and watched it slowly burn.

*

Down syndrome occurs through abnormal division of cells during pregnancy (specifically involving chromosome 21) and is almost never inherited. This is the chromosome that shapes certain physical features (eyes) and may affect developmental delays. Occasionally, the father or mother, exhibiting no outward symptoms or signs of the syndrome, can be a carrier and pass on extra genetic material through an unusual cell division process known as "translocation." But this is very rare. Down syndrome babies are usually born to women over forty as older eggs become especially vulnerable.

Early in the twentieth century, very few children with Down syndrome lived past the age of ten. Unless common complications such as heart defects and obesity become unusually severe, many people now live well into adulthood. Some of our campers had to get around at times with the assistance of a golf cart and were restricted from certain activities, but many returned each summer well into their fifties. We had "Hall of Fame" campers who'd been coming for twenty-five years or more and finally stopped not due to health challenges but from weariness with the overall camp regimen and daily schedule. I'm not sure I'd enjoy the experience at my age either.

My college major choice (and subsequent decision to enter seminary) was shaped by four summers with children and adults who had intellectual disabilities including Down syndrome. I loved them. They were unusually loyal—affectionate huggers who possessed scant penchant for posturing or pretense. When feelings got hurt, they got over any falling out quickly.

So many stories. A teenager named Sarge was obsessed with keeping our cabin tidy. He was the main reason we received a daily award from Mr. Clean after his secret inspections during swimming each afternoon. It was always refreshing how an affirming arrangement of sticker-stars on a paper plate could bring a person such joy. Sarge playfully barked out orders each morning. He told me more than once: "Remember, I'm the one in charge here." And, in many ways, he was.

Julie's letter revealed three things. She was pregnant and I was the father (no doubt there, she said). The baby most likely had Down syndrome. And she was keeping the child whether I wanted to be involved or not.

*

Fall at seminary turned toward winter. We even had an eight-inch snow that February, very unusual for South Carolina, crippling the city for a couple days. My friends and I borrowed lunch trays from the refectory and slid down steep hills in the park a couple blocks from campus, a welcome diversion from the rigors of hermeneutics class. I recall receiving a nice bruise just below my left knee that left me limping for several days after a long slide was interrupted by the stationary chain-basket pole normally serving as the tricky seventh hole for the park's Frisbee golf course.

Interpreting my role in Julie's predicament was usually (and blessedly) far from my mind that winter. I did think about telling Nancy once or twice, but knew such a revelation would devastate her. I also wasn't wild about a public transgression possibly reaching my synodical examining committee, a group of elders in the church who would eventually sign off on my ordination after perusing and probing topics ranging from cumulative GPA to dream life interpretation and anything in between. An older friend who'd recently graduated was actually asked if he ever had fantasies about his mother. Our wedding was scheduled for June, just before our departure for a year-long internship at a congregation in the North Carolina Piedmont.

I've noticed in my own ministry, thirty years out, how denial of personal responsibility involves a fascinating blend of creativity and deception that builds in intensity until one is usually cornered by the truth with no escape. Rare is the person who admits guilt when initially accused.

The Bible seems to contain two main schools of truth-telling. The prophet Jeremiah normally went straight for the moral jugular with the bold facts of the matter, often using visual aids such as a wooden neck-yoke in public worship, disrupting the comfortable Sabbath morning liturgy, or even his own buried underwear symbolizing unfaithful people who didn't cling closely to God anymore. Such direct honesty was tough on Jeremiah for the long haul. He wept almost weekly and, for his efforts on God's behalf, spent time in a cistern with mud up to his ass.

There's also the school of fidelity to the truth popularized by Jesus who told stories that rarely confronted people head-on but instead detonated down the road, perhaps hours later when the listener's guard wasn't up. I'm convinced that Jesus learned this artful narrative technique from his prophetic forebear, Nathan, who craftily advised King David during the years of his complicated monarchy. After the affair involving beautiful Bathsheba, the old prophet knew a direct confrontation with the wayward king could possibly get the messenger killed. Nathan tries another tack. A story about a wealthy man who takes what isn't his eventually traps David with the truth and leads to one of Scripture's most powerful penitential prayers: "Create in me a clean heart, O God, and put a new and right spirit within me."

My own evasion of the truth that winter was not terribly nuanced. Seminary served as a handy distraction. Crocus appeared in the park and our June plans became more steadily real. The wedding included several staff members from camp. Sarge even served as ring bearer and lined us all up at the rehearsal. The presiding pastor graciously smiled and stepped aside for the moment.

The year in North Carolina was everything we'd hoped. Without a hitch, I jumped through all the hoops leading to ordination, occasionally fearing, of course, that the truth might emerge in normal biblical fashion, direct or angular. But neither ever came.

*

After the rain, the sun peeks through low clouds on the horizon across the wide expanse of the lake. Reds and pinks color the western sky and purple martins play tag, lightly touching the water. A barred owl sounds on the opposite shore and I smile, recalling the rhyme we used in teaching campers to identify the call: *"Who cooks for you, who cooks for you-all?"*

I sit on the dock and consider heading back to the car. Nancy will worry, but the thought of putting on wet clothes invites a short lingering. The evening air warms a bit and I'm soon dry without a towel, careful to avoid worn parts of the wooden dock. A splinter lodged in an unusual location might take some explaining, a challenge surpassing the driving discomfort during the three-hour ride home.

Our marriage has been healthy and happy, for the most part, except for the inability to have children after many years of trying. Nancy still doesn't know my secret. Even though I've almost told her many times, it always seemed like the unburdening would be an unfair benefit to me and an additional wound for her.

During the lengthy and unsuccessful fertility counseling into our late thirties, the doctor printed out a two-page medical summary that made our heads swim with the various pregnancy risks. One word that leaped out on my genetic side of the spreadsheet was "translocation."

Nancy never pressed the doctor for a definition.

8.

Clergy Boy of Pennsylvania Avenue

PASTOR RANDY CLINTON STILL finds it hard to believe that he received a phone call from the White House. Certain it was a practical joke from one of his warped seminary classmates, Randy more than once asked, while laughing, "Now come on, who is this really?"

He even inquired if the caller might be "that sly bastard, Kevin Larsen," presently a Lutheran synodical bishop in the outback of South Dakota who graduated a year ahead of Randy at Luther Northwestern Bible Institute. That elicited a muffled and brief chuckle from the District of Columbia caller whose telephone ID was clearly nowhere near the center of America's winter tundra.

The upstate South Carolina pastor, nearing retirement and married to a local dentist, became convinced only after he thought to arrange a private Skype session between his church study laptop and the aide to the president who offered only his first name.

Speaking from within the spacious confines of the Oval Office, Mortimer's shoulders were framed by the famous bust of Martin Luther King, Jr., recently in the news for alleged (but ultimately false) removal by the new commander in chief, and a framed (but indeed bogus) *Time* magazine cover featuring his smiling boss receiving some prestigious award with a trademark "winning" pose. Senator Whimsy Graham, who grew up within shouting distance of Randy's church, talked softly in a corner behind Mortimer with a woman whom Randy did not recognize.

Randy almost called out to the senator, whom he'd met a few years back at the county Fall Oktoberfest, an annual weekend drunk featuring cotton candy, carnival rides, and a beer tent complete with authentic

German polka, celebrating the town's old homeland heritage. The festival also served as a favorite campaign stop for candidates seeking to strengthen their political base in a county voting Republican every presidential election since 1948, when Strom Thurmond briefly experimented with the Dixiecrats.

Under the tent, Randy had been talking with a Methodist colleague who went to high school with Whimsy when the senator sidled over with a tall cup of tepid Heineken and a small entourage of admirers. President Obama was seeking reelection the next month.

"Four words, gentlemen," drawled Whimsy, who could lapse into a southern accent when the moment called for one. "Pray your asses off." It didn't matter to the politician at that point that he was holding a Dutch brew instead of an authentic German lager, or that his emphatic theological imperative was rather slurred.

Randy wondered if Whimsy, still softly chatting with the woman in the background of his computer screen, might remember him and that bold invitation to sway God's presidential will with prayer.

But Mortimer was all business. "I hope, Pastor Clinton, that your initial reservations about our request are now sufficiently alleviated."

They weren't. "I have just one question," asked Randy, "with two parts. How in the world did you find me and why do you need a Lutheran to meet with the president?"

*

Many followers of the president's now-famous Twitter feed may not realize that his first cyber-crush continues to circle back to a near obsession with the homemade video efforts of common, salt-of-the-earth Americans found on YouTube.

This from the March issue of *People* magazine: "My youngest son wanted to post a vivid video description of his first masturbatory experience featuring teenage blow-up dolls living in the Rust Belt of Ohio and even though I thought the lad's creative juices were flowing mightily that evening (not to mention his pretty savvy adolescent political intuitions), I had to nix the video because CNN would undoubtedly try to make some sordid connection concerning the dysfunction of my little first family, even though this was just a little boy expressing himself. It's important, however, to slam the door early on warped public perception, and I think my son understands that."

The president was looking up the word *lascivious* in the dictionary one day, an adjective he heard Megyn Kelly use to describe him on "one of the shows" along with "lecherous," which led to a lingering perusal of many L-words, a pleasurable three-minute pause in an actual book, the first he'd held in his hands in the last eleven years. "I had no idea there was such a thing as a Lutheran and I want to know more about this little man, the theological populist who rocked all the dress-up homos in Rome way back when. Mortimer, find me a Lutheran pastor on YouTube."

And that, dear reader, is how the leader of the free world came to first hear about one Randy Clinton, aging pastor of First Lutheran Church in downtown Pine Barren, South Carolina.

*

Every winter, late in the Epiphany season just before the challenge of Lent, the saints at First Lutheran celebrate a rather over-the-top talent show that raises money for world hunger and serves as a Mardi Gras-like blowout for practicing Protestants who still observe the coming forty days with utmost spiritual rigor.

The talent show attracts a wide variety of guests ranging from the local Roman Catholic priest who has grown tired of his dour parishioners, overly focused on Marian devotional admonishment of even the most innocent fun, to a comical troupe of Iranian jugglers passing through Pine Barren for the annual county circus. One juggler—painted with a clown's makeup frown and clasping octogenarian Myrtle Owens like she was his best friend—was overheard to say that "these Lutherans really know how to throw a good party." (An aside: Myrtle later left town with this saucy Middle-Eastern man and has not been heard from since.)

One of the early videos posted on YouTube by the First Lutheran talent troupe known as the Epiphany Players was dubbed "The Bobbitt Sled," a curious cinematic coupling of the famous 1993 incident perpetrated by an angry wife, Lorena Bobbitt, with the XVII Olympic Winter Games held in Lillehammer, Norway, the following January. Pastor Randy was one of the lead writers.

In the church sketch, four bobsled teammates (all named John, the man with the severed member) attempt to board the slippery sled in a confused and stumbling katzenjammer while shouting at each other with the sober warning, "Don't cut me off!"

According to Mortimer as he spoke with Pastor Clinton that day during the Skype session, "The Bobbitt Sled" was a big hit with the president. "These Lutherans are absolutely crazy and exactly the kind of people that make this country great!" gushed the commander in chief. "This video is at least as salacious [an S-word recently mastered] as my *Access Hollywood* fiasco with Billy Bush, but you didn't hear of any censorship coming down on that pastor. I have to meet this guy and ask how he does it!"

But it was another YouTube video (a mere thirty-nine hits on the web) that really caught the attention of The White House, inspiring the president to ask his obedient aide, "I wonder if that guy might consider serving this great country as my pastor? His last name troubles me, but I think we can overlook that."

*

Part of the video's attraction, Mortimer admitted to Pastor Randy, was the talking she-ass from the book of Numbers. (Let the record show that even though the gender of this beast is ambiguous in various English translations, the original Hebrew clearly describes a female donkey who speaks forthrightly to a powerful man seemingly off the rails and intoxicated with his perceived self-importance. The reader should not attach undue metaphorical significance to the latter-day "donkey" who serves as the mascot for a major political party, but it's unquestionably difficult to know *exactly* what attracted the president—whose wild connective leaps of attention are legion—to this specific YouTube performance. Therefore, such an association should not be entirely ruled out. The words "she" and "ass" certainly aroused this powerful man, beloved by many millions more than any voting record shows.)

The popular *Left Behind* books, warning of the coming rapture of true believers, served as the central theme for the Epiphany Players that winter at First Lutheran Church. Comparing the surprise second coming of Christ to the days of Noah, the Bible ominously describes two souls working together in a field. "One will be taken and one will be left." Pastor Randy hated the books.

The talent show sketch, titled "Right Behind," depicts a group of men attending a support group for those afflicted with a large right butt-cheek.

Participants in the support group gather regularly to lament their respective "right bee-hinds." Helium balloons, stuffed down gym shorts, accentuate the affliction.

After much soul-searching and spirited sharing, the support group watches a taped segment featuring two Epiphany Players (posing as Old Testament scholars) whose skillful exegesis of the story of Balaam's Talking Ass brought down the house, especially Father Green, visiting that year's talent show from Saint Mary's Catholic Church.

The skit ends as the Right Bee-hinders, succored by the tale of the talking she-ass, watch the helium balloons "rapture" towards the fellowship hall ceiling. Freed from their embarrassment, the once-afflicted men engage in a circular lap-sit, with arms raised in freedom, while singing "Celebration" by Kool and the Gang.

Pastor Randy confessed bewilderment to Mortimer that it had taken this long for the YouTube video to catch someone's eye. Thirty-nine hits were something of an embarrassment. But he never dreamed a country's actual head-of-state might find these Lutheran antics nearly as funny as he did. One livid viewer, a retired Methodist bishop from Kansas, phoned Randy several years ago and vowed to have him defrocked. Mortimer, who wasn't used to laughing, chuckled softly as the Skype session concluded.

"I have to meet that man," said the president of Randy. "If his personality at all matches his first name then I want to have him full time here on Pennsylvania Avenue."

*

One afternoon in Pine Barren, a limousine pulled up to the parsonage on Main Street, attracting the stares of Randy's neighbors who quickly called many of their friends with the news. Gawkers gathered on the sidewalk as Mortimer and the president, surrounded by several armed Secret Service agents, climbed the steps to the front porch and entered a rather nice living room furnished by the excellent dental skills of Randy's wife, Ella.

Here he was, big as life, out with the common people where he loved to be. A gentle South Carolina breeze blew a large shock of hair out of place, combed back with the important man's elfishly small left hand.

Randy, still grieving his mother's death from two weeks earlier, was nevertheless glad she was not present that day in the living room. His mom, with progressive dementia, had started offering loud (and sometimes profane) comments in public on the girth of heavy people struggling with their weight. "Would you look at the stomach on that one!" she called out recently at the local steak house. Randy had learned to time the loud judgments from his mom with an even louder cough to mask the embarrassment, and was relieved she was not present to render a judgment on the ample waistline of the commander in chief.

The president got right to the point. "Here's the deal," he said. "I like you. I don't like many people, but you I like. You're funny. You're a winner. Jesus was all about winning so I'm offering you a sweet salary to get in my car out there, right now, and come be my Clergy Boy in Washington. Or, whatever you call yourself. It doesn't matter."

"Wear your little clerical shirt, pass out the crackers on Sunday, and say amusing things from Two Corinthians when called upon—you know, funny it up. That big black best seller is way too serious. The people of this country don't want a downer of a Savior. What was God thinking anyway with that nutty wooden cross idea? That thing you did with the talking she-ass, which reminded me a lot of Hillary. Now *that* was funny. What do you say?"

Silence filled the room, awkwardly. "Can I call you tomorrow morning, Mr. President?"

"Absolutely, but please call me Donnie. All my friends do."

The entourage consumed three pecan pies and a gallon and a half of lemonade. Pastor Randy closed the front door of the parsonage and waited for his phone to ring.

*

The streets of Pine Barren are unusually quiet just before dawn. Pastor Randy slipped silently out of the house for his morning jog. The previous evening had been hectic and exhausting as camera crews from two nearby television stations explored every conceivable angle of the president's invitation, including Ella's thoughts on how her husband's possible acceptance might affect the overall health and direction of her dental practice.

The Bible is full of dreams and various dreamers, but Randy's fifteen-minute snatches of anything resembling sleep the night before kept returning to the single-minded faithfulness of Daniel, exiled far from home in a foreign land and known chiefly for his courage in a den of lions, a story that might serve Randy well in his possible new call as the president's pastor.

However, it was Daniel's shrewd interpretations of the vivid dream life of King Nebuchadnezzar that finally convinced Randy. In chapter four of the book bearing his name, the young prophet dares to speak forthrightly concerning royal nightmares spawned by the king's shameful abuse of power and negligence of the oppressed. Daniel interprets the king's colorful dream to mean that he'll be taken down a notch or two, eating grass like an ox in the field and bathing "with the dew of heaven." The young exile's prophecy comes true. The king was driven from his opulence "until his hair grew as long as eagles' feathers and his nails became like birds' claws."

The commander in chief kept his nails trimmed nicely, but his feathery hair needed a good bit of work. Randy laughed out loud at that idea during his jog. Perhaps he could use these old stories like a subtle mirror reflecting God's discipline for a cocky and arrogant man.

Randy walked the last block leading back to the parsonage. The sun was just coming up. He smelled bacon frying through a neighbor's open kitchen window. He loved this little town. The pastor entered his house and found Ella eating directly from a carton of yogurt with a dental instrument.

"Okay, I'll try it," he said. "For six months." Randy looked at the woman he loved. Being apart until December and commuting between Pine Barren and the nation's capital wouldn't be so bad.

They prayed together, then Randy said, "The guy's crazy. We all know that. But maybe he needs God more than most."

*

It didn't surprise Randy that Mortimer had already collected a rather thick dossier of very minor indiscretions spanning his thirty-year clerical career. But its existence became especially wearisome whenever the little man raised his eyebrows in mock surprise during Randy's pointed Monday morning staff devotionals, suggesting with a sly grin that all of the pastor's secrets could be conveniently revealed at any time.

Mortimer especially seemed to detest the prophet Amos, so Randy decided to turn up the heat, fully aware of the recent furniture delivery to the executive residence. "Alas for those who lie on beds of ivory, and lounge on their couches." The president, away at Mar-a-Lago for a long weekend, would surely hear about the latest pastoral impropriety upon his return.

Mortimer thought to himself: "Who does this uppity preacher think he is, quoting some obscure nut-case sycamore tree farmer living eight centuries prior to Christ Almighty!"

The "Manual of Manipulation," as Randy called it privately with Ella, included two incidents from early in his ministry that didn't bother Randy in the slightest. The first occurred in 1986 on a confirmation retreat. Well after midnight, Pastor Randy heard raucous laughter in the street outside his bedroom window. Finding only one sheepish-looking teenager in the cabin who wouldn't speak, Randy opened the front door in his pajamas and saw young Sally (age fifteen) riding bareback astride a shirtless young man named Clarence. A bright street lamp illumined the pair with four other fully clothed adolescents in pursuit. All the youth were drunk except for the quivering and mum girl inside the house. They'd broken into the lake house liquor cabinet.

Randy called all the parents at 5:00 AM and led a Bible study based upon the Prodigal Son. If Mortimer wanted to leak this incident to the press, it was clear the pastor's personal self-defense could be impeccably offered.

The second incident, which Mortimer seemed to relish even more than the first, involved a former youth minister at Randy's church from his days in "The Commonwealth," as the little presidential aide enjoyed saying, presumably since he lived across the Potomac with all the other snooty citizens of Alexandria. Randy did indeed shiver a bit when Mortimer played this dated file card from an era when parents probably broached intimate topics of human sexuality a bit early with their young children. This had certainly been the case with Randy, who enjoyed reading with his young son a lavishly illustrated children's book, *Where Did I Come From?*, which featured a graphic series of naked fat people describing the basics of human reproduction, including one memorable description of the male orgasm: "much like a tickly sneeze." Ella more than once mentioned to Randy that their son was probably not quite ready for such mature exposure to the facts of life.

The youth minister, later fired by Randy's Virginia congregation, made the mistake one Sunday afternoon of soliciting from the teenagers a variety of slang expressions commonly associated with both male and female genitalia. These words were left unerased on the large blackboard in the basement youth room and discovered by one Mabel Thornton, a pillar of the congregation, who'd returned the next morning to search the premises for her missing handbag.

Mortimer had somehow obtained a photograph of the chalky list that now resided in Randy's aforementioned file. The president especially enjoyed looking at this embarrassing bevy of titillating expressions, asking to see the list more than once and particularly resting his focus upon the phrase "muff dive," which made the jowly leader laugh uproariously. "I like this pastor!" he roared, missing the point entirely that the blackboard compendium was someone else's indiscretion, not Randy's.

*

Two months into his experimental call to the White House, Pastor Randy continued to sense things were not going so well. He missed the people of Pine Barren and intensely pined for Ella, even her frequent reminders to floss.

But the main worry, even eclipsing Mortimer's peevish nature: the many calls in the middle of the night from a president who never seemed to sleep. The phone rang at completely unpredictable intervals, usually starting after 2:00 AM.

An example: "Hey, Rev, I think you know who this is. I'm about to send out a group tweet to my former wives telling them they all look pretty fat now. Is there anything in the Bible about lard? I was looking through the big book at all the 3:16s and saw the one in Leviticus about 'all fat' belonging to the Lord. What did old Levi mean by that? Do you think that verse might fit these horsefaces? I don't want to be overly harsh here because these porkers are also the mothers of my children. So, I need to wedge a little God into my criticism here. You know, so that bastard Jake Tapper won't have a field day on TV and say I'm crazy."

The pastor tried valiantly to listen as the weeks went by, feeling that his small role as theological advisor might indeed sway public perception of a man mired in constant conflict. Randy summoned patience from a deep well of experience. The president was not the first strong personality he'd encountered in three decades of relatively odd work.

One morning Randy passed Mortimer in a West Wing hallway. The little man was grinning like a Cheshire cat. "The president would like to see you now," he cooed.

Behind his desk in the large swivel chair, with his back turned to the pastor, the commander in chief rested his chin upon raised index fingers in a position that resembled a pointed gun. A full thirty seconds passed with neither man speaking.

"Randy . . . I can call you Randy now, right? We're old friends." The president's chair did not move, angled toward the window. He looked across the bushes at the expansive lawn where his young son was playing a spirited game of croquet with two Secret Service men. More silence. The chair finally swiveled toward the waiting pastor. The president had tears in his eyes.

"I've struggled with this decision," said the man whose tangerine hair that morning was unusually unkempt. "I've prayed for about ten seconds and even phoned the son of my dad's old pastor, 'Stormin' Norman Vinnie,' my Pop used to call him."

Randy almost laughed, suppressing a smile upon noticing the president's anguish. Mortimer peeked his head into the Oval Office and was quickly shooed away with an impatient (and also rather smallish) right hand and the words, "Would you leave us the fuck alone, Mortie?" This did elicit a laugh from the pastor who knew what was coming even though he'd never seen a single episode of the famous television show.

"Randy, I'm gonna have to let you go. In many ways, you've been a godsend around here. You've always answered your phone in the middle of the night and those sweet little prayers prior to all our fast-food meals from Burger King sounded just like Billy Graham. But it's too much Bible, Randy. My God, you really take the damn book seriously, don't you? I have to hand this to you. I've never known all that shit about serving the poor was even in there and, frankly, if I kept you on here much longer you might even have me believing all that crap. You're fired, Randy. You're the first pastor I've ever fired, but honestly, you're the first pastor I've really ever had so that's not sayin' much, is it?"

The president rose, smiling, the tears now drying but visible. "I'm gonna miss you Randy. If you ever need anything, call me."

*

Retirement in a place like Pine Barren, South Carolina, is not as uneventful as you might think. Seasonal parades wind alongside the old parsonage that Randy and Ella bought from the good people at First Lutheran. Friends drop by for a piece of Randy's famous peach pie and reminisce about churches in other locales where they were once together. Ella decided to work a few more years as a dentist but admits in a moment of unedited honesty that she's tired of peering into the mouths of children whose attention to the basics of oral health is frankly atrocious.

An occasional reporter makes a front porch appointment with Randy to reflect upon the pastor's tenure in the White House and ask him why the president hasn't bothered to call a new minister to Washington for the man's surprising second term.

Randy thinks for a while before answering, waiting for the clatter of playing cards pinned to bicycle spokes to pass on the front sidewalk and slowly die away in the distance. He knows he could tell the reporter any number of amusing stories about the man's pomposity and disregard for the holy.

But instead the old pastor chooses his words judiciously, and slowly describes a church member from his first parish, a pharmacist named Jim, who would take time to pray with the old women who brought their problems to his pharmacy window at Walmart. The prayers were short and to the point, not filled with much theological nuance. "But Jim was trying," said Randy, "trying to live out his faith even when that small act of grace almost cost him his job."

"The president prayed as he was able," Randy said. "That's about all I can tell you about anybody, including one of the most powerful men on the planet. Maybe he knows deep down that prayer can change a person. And if you want to know the truth, I'm not sure he wants to change all that much. Not many people do."

The reporter thanked Randy for his time and for the peach pie. She promised to send him a draft of the newspaper article for his input and approval prior to publication. She already had a title for the article: "Pastor to the Prez." She asked what he thought.

"I hope more than anything that he somehow reads it. God knows the man still needs a pastor."

9.

The Watchmaker's Apprentice

EVEN IN THE RAIN, the little boy stands on a small stool, motionless, in an unpaved alley behind the shop on Rosewood Drive. He is just tall enough to see an old man working on the other side of the glass window with an array of tools and spare parts spread out on his workbench like pieces of glittering gold and silver. When school lets out for the summer, the boy arrives each morning precisely at 8:00 AM after a half-mile walk from home, steps on the stool, and observes the watchmaker through the window, small hands resting on the pane's wooden ledge for balance.

Cats chase mice down the alley. Bicycles blast by. Children shout. But the boy's gaze remains riveted upon the man's dexterous and precise fingers that glide across the table as if conducting a miniature orchestra. No words are ever exchanged and rarely any eye contact, except the occasional glance or nod to make sure the boy has seen the last tricky maneuver accomplished with tweezers and a tiny coiled spring.

Unlike others his age, the boy is capable of a steady, focused stare for hours at a time, as if peering into another world, even as neighborhood kids call out names he doesn't seem to hear. Not the last taunts aimed at a diminutive frame that never quite reaches four feet, even as an adult. The boy reluctantly steps down from the stool twenty minutes before noon, only because his mom expects him for lunch.

*

I glance out at him between communion tables from the high neo-gothic altar at Memorial Lutheran Church in downtown Springfield, South

80

Carolina. He greets communicants returning to their respective pews after receiving Christ's body and blood. They dip one hand in the water, signing a moist cross on their foreheads, and he grabs the other hand in both of his.

Julian stands on a small stool near the baptismal font in the center aisle of the nave. After so many decades at this sacramental post, his greeting has become as much a fixed part of the weekly liturgy as the absolution. Beloved by all, Julian's the ecclesiastical mascot for Memorial members, a role I discourage but one he indulges and even embraces.

Turning towards the cross on the east wall of the chancel, I mask a low laugh. He honestly resembles an elfin lawn ornament. Revealing mismatched socks, rolled-up pants call out for dry cleaning. A tattered necktie that badly needs replacing—bearing the pattern of an American flag, worn every Sunday—hangs well below his waist. I doubt anyone present would ever guess the secret Julian keeps, its weight leading him here each week to his smiling perch on the small stool.

*

The front door of Julian's house is almost hidden in a jumble of ivy and vines. I have a hard time finding the knocker and squeeze through hanging vegetation after he finally answers. He leads me back to his kitchen through an obstacle course of newspapers, stacks of old *Playboy* magazines, and so much junk that brother Johnny's declaration describing Julian as a hoarder seems rather understated. There's hardly anywhere to sit.

I tell Julian that I've been a bit worried about him, especially since hearing of his seven-mile hike (one way) from Elmwood cemetery where his car died at his mother's grave, during his weekly visit for extended conversation and advice. Julian's an excellent self-taught mechanic. Even at eighty-two, he's able to shimmy his small body into tight spots under the hood that would be challenging for a chipmunk. Johnny, who lives next door, tells me it's not unusual to see most of his brother's wiry body buried somewhere in the engine's guts with a bare foot raised skyward like a small flag.

The trunk of Julian's old 1963 Ford Fairlane—laden with hundreds of tinkering tools including an impressive array of unmatched screwdrivers found roadside during long walks around town—comically sags and leaves an alarmingly low ground clearance. He's been known to walk to the corner station with a gas can and purchase a single gallon at a time, carefully recording exact mileage traveled until it's time for another. "That young 'un can pinch a penny until it yells for mercy," Johnny once said.

Julian wouldn't call a wrecker or a cab that day upon failing to locate the proper trunk tool. He walked home. And after stowing what he needed in a deep overalls pocket, walked back to the cemetery in the rain, fixed the car while holding a small flashlight in his teeth, finally arriving at his little bungalow on Straight Street well after dark. He didn't forget to say goodbye to his mom for another week, also asking her to forgive the flurry of curse words he offered to the Lord on his little fourteen-mile junket, impressive for anyone but especially noteworthy for a dwarf.

"There's no need to worry about me, Pastor," he called over his shoulder from the next room on a quick errand to throw a bedsheet over the *Playboys*. "Pour yourself a mug of tea from the stove. I think it's apple-cinnamon brewin' today. You might need to wash yourself a mug." I was happy to oblige after noticing mouse traps all over the kitchen, one holding a rodent whose hind legs were still faintly wiggling.

Julian's entire house, small as it is, has twice been condemned by the city for lack of upkeep, a topic best avoided unless you're prepared to hear him hold forth for the next hour about "the inept staff of hoodlums at the mayor's office" and the repeated hundred-dollar fines he's had to pay over the years.

I suspect Julian never really missed the cash. If the rumors are true, he's one of the richest people in the city.

*

A friend of mine got a call from his nephew in New Jersey the other day. "Uncle Chris," he said, breathlessly, "you're not going to believe it. You and Aunt Carolyn need to come up and see this." After Chris's mom died last October, the nephew moved into the old home place in a middle-class neighborhood once brimming with German immigrants. He was throwing away several decades of old cleaning supplies under the kitchen sink and found a hidden cache of plastic grocery bags jammed into a hole in the wall.

The bags were full of cash, some filled with very wet cash. No bag contained more than a hundred dollars, but when Chris and the nephew laid it out to dry on counters all over the kitchen, they counted almost 150,000 dollars. Mom had been stuffing most of her weekly allowance under the sink for decades. Chris told me she never seemed to have any money but did say once with a twinkle, "You're going to find a little surprise one day when I'm gone."

She's not the first Depression Era octogenarian I've known who's hidden money. On seminary internship in the North Carolina mountains, I met parishioners who wedged their life savings under cabin floorboards, often surprising children who always thought their daddy was broke. My own mother stashes a couple thousand in what she calls "the freezer bank" in her assisted living apartment across town, and dips into the icy vault only when she needs some handy bills for a grandchild's birthday card.

Julian angrily closed his checking account a couple years back because they kept charging him fees for dipping under a minimum balance. "They're crooks," he told me. "Every last one of them."

*

I've never known many dwarves and certainly none as well as Julian. That character on *Game of Thrones* seems to attract his share of women, but Johnny tells me that Julian has never had a girlfriend, not even close. "There's this woman—she looks like a young hobo—who comes by every other month or so. I know he gives her money but don't ask me what they do together when they go inside his little house. There's not enough room in there to wiggle. You know it's true."

The Bible describes giants (Goliath, of course) and other strapping souls like Samson in the book of Judges and the famous Nephilim in Genesis, but no heroic dwarves. The book of Leviticus even specifically forbids people like Julian from ordination into the Aaronic priesthood along with "hunchbacks and those with crushed testicles."

As a younger man, I had an orchiectomy (look it up) after a brush with cancer, but it's a bit more challenging to check that sort of blemish at the door of the church. Our church treasurer, an amusing man who knows my surgical history, once offered a high compliment after a sermon when I challenged our reluctant congregation to tithe. "That takes ball, man," he said.

Julian doesn't talk about it with me, but I suspect he considers his size some sort of frowning judgment from God: "The Divine Watchmaker who wound up the world and created the whole ball of wax," he once said on a Wednesday in Lent during a time for church member testimonials. Julian used the story of Zacchaeus—the wily little tax collector who climbed the sycamore tree to get a better glimpse of Jesus—as his scriptural basis that evening. The church was packed, unusual for a Wednesday night. Beaming, he stood beside me at the door of the church and greeted people after the service. Gladys Barnett, an opinionated crone who's never had an unspoken thought, told Julian that she always thought of the actor Danny DeVito whenever she heard Zacchaeus's name. I noticed that Julian didn't appreciate the comparison.

After everyone left that night, I told Julian that several early church commentators thought Jesus was actually the small man and the tree-climbing occurred because the Lord was almost hidden in the large crowd by much taller people. A close examination of the Greek pronouns referring to the two men suggests delightful ambiguity in this regard. Julian wasn't buying it. "I know all that about divinity working through tiny sources like mustard seeds, but the Son of God was no little person like me. He wouldn't have lasted an hour on that cross, much less three."

*

Julian was absent one Sunday morning not long after Easter. I knew that could only mean he was sick, or maybe dead. Our associate pastor found Emily Harris in her living room recliner last year with a smile on her face. The coroner said she'd been dead at least three days. Julian never missed church. I drove over to Straight Street after greeting a long line of parishioners who all wanted to know about him.

Honeysuckle vine almost entirely covered the doorway. I've always loved that sweet smell. As a child, I thought it was possible to collect a Mason jar full of nectar with a little patience and charge enough per cup to make my friend's lemonade stand look pretty lame. I tried to peer through the smudged square of glass at the top of the door.

Nobody answered as hummingbirds flitted around the blossoms. The Fairlane was gone. Johnny (indeed sick that Sunday with what sounded like the flu) peeked out his own front door and said, "I haven't seen that young 'un since yesterday afternoon. Wasn't he in church? Something's wrong, Pastor. Should we check the hospital?"

Even with HIPAA laws protecting privacy, the staff at Springfield Health Care still slips me information on the sly, given my longevity in town. Oddly, two people were listed under Julian's last name in the maternity wing of the hospital.

I saw him halfway down the third-floor hallway, standing on a small stool, looking through the window at the babies. His hands rested on the pane's long sill for balance. Without turning his head, he spoke, perhaps recognizing my reflection in the glass but maybe not. His focus, legendary since the days of gazing at the watchmaker through the alley glass, remained rapt and straight ahead. I suspect a bomb would not have dislodged him from his perch.

"Sort of thought you might be here this afternoon," he said. "If you've got a few minutes, they might let you hold him." Julian still had not looked my way. "Isn't he about the most beautiful thing you've ever seen?"

*

Johnny was indeed rather prescient when he said he couldn't imagine what his brother was doing in the cottage with "that hobo woman." Nobody else could believe it either. Her name is Susan. She's almost thirty but could pass for a lot younger. I don't want to push the analogy too far, of course, but I couldn't help but think of Mary's unusual pregnancy, thought by many to be a teenager when Jesus was born with a much-older Joseph standing faithfully by her side throughout the ordeal.

People talked, as church folk will, especially when the three of them moved into the cottage together on Straight Street. Susan hardly had anything to move. A corner of the cottage was cleared of debris for a crib. The church women dutifully delivered meals for a week and took turns rocking the baby. Julian donated his *Playboy* collection to his pastor, believe it or not. I didn't have the heart to tell him I burned them all with our autumn leaves, noticing Miss July's bosom wilting in the flames as my wife stood on the back porch with her arms folded.

*

The church was full the Sunday baby James was baptized early that winter in the Epiphany season. Julian stood on his familiar stool near the font. Susan still towered over him by at least a foot. Julian held little James throughout the service. That baby never made a peep, staying awake the whole time with a steady gaze that looked right at me even when the water was poured over his head from the baptism shell.

The Bible text that morning was the story of Jesus turning water into wine. Some interpretive accounts from the early church suggest that not only the stone jars but also the entire well became filled with the new and sparkling life.

It wasn't hard to make a sermonic connection between the Bible story and the new scholarship fund Julian named in honor of his son. A million-dollar principal would assist a lot of needy kids in our community for decades to come. Much of the money had been stashed in the two rear panels of the Fairlane. More was buried in a metal canister at the foot of his mother's grave over at Elmwood Cemetery.

*

Susan decided to stay in the little cottage when Julian died the next year, even though she surely could have afforded something nicer. She did clean the tangled mess off the porch and planted a flower garden out front. James usually totters close behind with his plastic trowel.

Sometimes during the week I'll walk into the church when nobody's there and pray in the last light of the afternoon. Unlike Julian, my mind's focus wanders to a hundred different things.

I close my eyes and recall the song of the seraphs who beckon Isaiah to notice God's holiness infiltrating the whole earth full. Leaving the church sanctuary, heading home, I pick up a small screwdriver somebody has left near the font. Up near the altar, I hear the flutter of wings.

10.

Eclipsalypse

I'VE NEVER BEEN ONE to embrace hype. My wife Susan's students have all been issued the special viewing glasses to shield youthful eyes. Many are using the day to stay at home and pretend they're interested in science.

Why all this attention for a couple minutes out of one day when every single day brings fresh surprises of wonder if you'd just open your eyes? I'd planned to board my bicycle in the nude as a sort of protest and ride up and down our road under the cover of dark totality. The police cars usually stationed at either end to curb speeders (the west end T-stopping at the middle school) have helped me rethink the idea even though fairly long stretches allowing a gentle coast in third gear are generally forested.

A friend in Maine wrote. "It really wouldn't look that great for a naked retired Lutheran minister to be apprehended by local law enforcement officers so close to a school building. Your goal of experiencing the full-body moon shadow is laudable, but I recommend locating a large clearing in your nearby national forest. You do know your county chapter of 'Wiccans for Jesus' will probably conduct a nude solstice dance around an evening bonfire next June. Have you considered waiting a few months to publicly disrobe with others? It's difficult to arrest a naked crowd. You'll recall the campus streaking craze back in our college days when the cops just gave up."

He's probably right but I haven't ruled out my ride in the altogether quite yet. Susan says it might be rather embarrassing to be surrounded by headlight illumination from the aging Bonneville driven by our neighbor, Betty, who might be moved to purchase an emergency gallon of milk at Ingle's during the apex of the celestial event.

"Pastor, I've always wondered what you looked like under that robe." I could handle that and Betty could use a little excitement in her life. But I predict there won't be anyone out on the roads before (or during) totality and plan to test that prediction later this morning.

On the phone yesterday, my father-in-law reported that residents in his town are renting spaces on their lawns for Midwestern tent campers descending like a swarm of locusts upon our prime viewing sky-band in upstate South Carolina. It reminds me of renting out one's home for a NASCAR race where we once lived—close to the Virginia-Tennessee border and Bristol's famous banked half-mile.

What is it about snazzy spectacle that attracts all the nuts like a magnet? I posed this question to Susan last night and she looked at me with a thin smile (no teeth showing) and raised eyebrows, never answering.

The Harry Potter phenomenon similarly confuses me. The books are well-written, but why relinquish your whole life to the narrative? Does one really need to expend gobs of cash dressing exactly like Dumbledore on Halloween to feel authentic and alive? Answer these questions, please.

6:45 AM

Dad just called. The residents at my father's nursing home ten miles away plan to line up on the back porch of Riverside Cottage to view the event from a row of rocking chairs accompanied with stems of Chardonnay. I want a picture of that. Octogenarians in their special viewing spectacles, looking skyward from their rockers with measured oscillation. Dad says, "After breakfast, I think I'll just hide under the covers until it's over."

I understand such sentiment, but it's an uncovering that gets my juices flowing. I once ran through a graveyard naked on the Appalachian Trail with a good friend. Our wives—eating lunch near a tombstone dating back to early settlers in the Shenandoah Valley—heard the approaching clomp of our hiking boots, but refused to look up. Their loss.

7:40 AM

Susan heads out the door for school. Not the school up the hill just a half-mile away, but the new high school recently carved out of a large piece of land along scenic Highway 11 near Pickett Post. She teaches English and plans to center classes for the day upon the big event. Requiring two trips from den to driveway and her Honda CRV, Susan packs several large quilts for her students' reclined viewing pleasure, scheduled this afternoon for the football field. "Won't you drive out to the school and join us around two?"

She still looks beautiful, after thirty-six years of marriage, in the open doorway of the new morning. I always tend to disappoint her with my stubborn refusals. Adolescents unnerve me, especially since our three have grown into young adults. Reliving the horror gives me the shivers. We kiss goodbye and I promise to rethink the nude cycling during the eclipse, just to keep her guessing, even though I've already mostly decided against it.

After morning Bible reading, over breakfast of granola and a hard-boiled egg, I discover that ancient Vikings believed the sun and moon were being eaten during an eclipse by two ravenous wolves, Hati and Skoll. The names mean "One Who Hates" and "One Who Mocks," respectively. I never knew hatred and mockery could translate to such voracious lunar and solar appetites, but there you have it. The two beasts remind me of a novel I once read where the main character eats an entire automobile in small bites over several years. The Norse *canis lupus* must have an impressive digestive lineage.

I feel bloated but keep reading. In February of 1831, Nat Turner interpreted a winter eclipse as a black man reaching for the sun, clear grounds for the revolt he'd lead later that year in August. His call to arms conflicts with Herodotus, the Greek historian, who reports how the celestial alignment brought an end to war between the Lydians and Medes just over half a millennium before Christ, who in turn foresaw something like an eclipse when he predicted "the sun will be darkened and the moon will not give its light" after a certain tribulation suffered by all true believers. I used to love preaching on that one just before Christmas, and told my parishioners that Lutherans were never more out of step during the year than at Advent. Now retired, I can be out of step anytime.

Anyway, given the various conflicting eclipse quips offered by the likes of Nat, Herodotus, and Jesus, it's only fair to formulate my own and that will require nudity in some form. I think more clearly when naked.

10:35 AM

In the half hour spent on my bicycle (fully clothed) in a leisurely investigative foray along nearby roads and lanes, I encountered, as expected, exactly four moving vehicles. Several possible conclusions: 1) Everybody's home because they've chosen to take Eclipse Monday off; 2) People have started drinking, deciding to mix moon-gazing with a little local moonshine; 3) Countywide Christians, with proven conservative theological sensibilities, prefer their Jesus sprinkled with a strong side serving of apocalyptic and have already started to hunker down inside; or 4) Possibly a mixture of all three.

Susan answers my texted cycling report between classes. "See? There's no traffic. You'll have a straight shot out to the football field at two. Please come."

I'm evasive, offering a lie about late summer ragweed allergies, which does not hold up for long since I've just dismounted the bike. She does seem to buy my excuse of needing a shower. I'm sweating after the ride in the early South Carolina heat, water dripping off my body like a small tributary of the Chattooga River.

As I wipe off sweat in the garage with an old cloth, a bird barks from the limb of an old oak tree in the front yard. Yes, oddly, it barked. This day is getting stranger by the hour.

12:47 PM

Despite the heat, it's a beautiful day in the upstate. Surrounded by lawn and garden tools, I notice a slight darkening of the sky while eating a peanut butter and jelly sandwich on a small stool in the open garage. Experiencing the full wonder of the eclipse will require sharpened senses fueled by the protein rush of legumes.

Sitting on the stool, I recall how much cutting grass pleases an aging pastor. The lushness and deep emerald green of Palisades Zoysia (developed by one Dr. Milt Engelke at Texas A&M) excite me more than most. Unlike church work, I'm able to detect immediate results via the crisp mowing patterns, regimented trimming sequences, and gentle pulses of the cordless blower.

Susan once jokingly said she needs to exit the premises and go shopping during these lawn chores because "you always finish with an obvious Yard-On." She teaches English; that saucy lass can certainly turn a phrase.

Our cat, scampering after a field mouse in the corner of the garage, just laughed. Yes, she laughed. A distinct feline chuckle. I choose to associate the sound with the rare coming alignment of sun and moon. Everyone else and their uncle seem to be making absurd connections with the approaching darkness. Why not I?

2:15 PM

A loud voice sounds over the trees and, for a second, I've forgotten that the middle school children are all assembled in nearby stands overlooking the athletic fields. The school is about a quarter-mile away by road but the stadium is much closer as the crow flies. And said bird is indeed flying over the trees as the normally cacophonous cicadas begin an eerie afternoon lull while darkness continues to fall. It almost sounds like the insects are whispering to each other and saying, "Hush, hush, hush, hush."

"KEEP YOUR GLASSES ON UNTIL I GIVE THE WORD," booms the voice over a public-address system. I assume the man-voice is either the principal or a science teacher. Hundreds of children laugh and shout, expectant and excited. "YOU CAN LOSE YOUR SIGHT IF YOU STARE DIRECTLY AT THE PARTIAL ECLIPSE. WAIT UNTIL I GIVE THE ALL-CLEAR BEFORE REMOVING THE GLASSES. AND THIS ESPECIALLY MEANS YOU, ETHAN."

I'm smiling broadly in the garage, but also sucking air through clenched teeth, recalling what one of our church members, a middle school math teacher, told me about an unruly child with the same name. Even for an imp like Ethan, it must be tough getting called out like that in front of the whole school. Sort of like the voice of God from on high.

No one in a car (or on foot) has appeared in front of our house for at least the last hour. The whole town is now perched somewhere watching the sky. I could easily hop on the bike and make it, sans clothing, to the end of the road and back in the projected duration for totality.

The word *totality* in conjunction with imagined nudity amuses me for a moment. *Totally naked.* I could add this venue to my list of previous and unique birthday-clothed sites.

At a Lutheran summer camp when I was in college, a dozen of us packed into a van and rode up to the Blue Ridge Parkway on a beautiful Saturday evening. No kids and no moon. We parked at an isolated overlook above Asheville. I can't remember who issued the challenge but the six guys agreed to streak down the Parkway first for a hundred yards only if the six girls would follow suit in their own birthday suits. After the nude male dash, they chickened out and scampered down the mountain road in bras and panties, so my friend Charles got behind the wheel of the van and followed them in the headlights as the screaming girls veered like frightened deer into the scratchy shadows of a mountain laurel thicket.

Returning to camp, someone broke our vow of silence in the dining hall at breakfast. The camp director, Pastor Rob, got wind of the group-streak and called a serious midnight meeting for all twelve perpetrators that same Sunday night. He looked grave and rather stern, holding a Bible, as we sat in an arranged semicircle in the cavernous meeting room outside his office.

"I don't have to tell you how this would look in the newspapers if Luther Glen Summer Camp counselors were arrested streaking on the Blue Ridge Parkway." He seemed to be looking at me more than the others, for some reason.

No one spoke. My friend Sharon finally broke the silence. "Pastor Rob," she said, eyes filling with tears and arms folded across her chest. "It's not what you think. I've never felt this close to any other Christian friends in my entire life. And never so close to the Lord. So, I'm not sure what *you're* thinking, but it wasn't that."

It's getting even darker. At the last moment, I decide my friend from Maine is sensibly prudent, especially after I tiptoe to the middle of the road (why stealth at this point?) and notice the outline of a parked police car at the stop sign in the distance. The patrolman's emergency flashers cease spinning and go dark.

The bike idea just won't work. Susan would die a thousand deaths if she had to bail her pastor-husband out of the county detention center. Another idea comes to mind.

Heading back towards the house, I almost step on a blacksnake slithering across the road. Shadows deepen and the line of trees bordering our property almost vanishes.

2:36 PM

Totality.

Last night I investigated the NASA website and learned that our area would receive almost three full minutes of darkness. Plenty of time.

The middle school students across the tall pine trees are quiet as church mice. Not a peep on our road. No crickets. No birdsong. Silence.

Already shirtless, I step out of my gym shorts, toss the balled under-wear back over my left shoulder towards the garage, and walk barefooted (and bare-bodied) to our side yard where we've planted a small vegetable garden. The damp loose earth between the rows feels good on my toes. Zuc-chini and squash vines look like they're moving and twisting in the shadow.

I lock ten fingers behind my head and arch shoulders backward, rais-ing eyes towards the black moon. A thin shimmering light circles its edge. I think about the magical synchronicity of this moment. I think of Susan and her students, reclining on quilts a few miles away at the football field. I think of young Ethan across the trees and wonder if this upward gaze can finally capture his wayward attention. I think of Hati and Skoll and Nat Turner and Jesus. A lot can amble through a person's mind in three minutes, especially one as cluttered as mine.

Mostly I look. I read recently that nine galaxies exist in the cosmos for every human being on our planet. That's a lot of galaxies. And we're spinning through just one.

"When I look at your heavens, the work of your fingers, the moon and the stars that you have established; what are human beings that you are mindful of them, mortals that you care for them?" A prayer, an old and beautiful psalm, attributed to David. The eighth. I speak the words aloud and wonder if the psalmist was also nude at the time, looking up.

2:39 PM

The light begins its slow return. Time to head back to the garage and put on some shorts.

"WHERE ARE YOU?"

The voice over the trees again. It must be awesome to have such moral authority over the behavior of so many impressionable young people, shap-ing adolescents into hopefully respectable citizens.

"WHAT HAVE YOU DONE?"

I initially wonder if Ethan is in trouble again and may have fried his rebellious eyes by removing the glasses too soon. What an impudent little cuss he must be.

But as light returns, I notice that the entire landscape that was once my neighborhood has drastically changed. The house I live in is not there anymore. The front yard is filled with beautiful trees and friendly animals and exotic birds and a snake, walking upright.

A woman who is not my wife is pointing at me, seeming to assign some sort of blame. (My God, is she ever gorgeous.)

We are both wearing strategically located leaves from some local tree, but I sense the outfit is a rather recent addition to our garden wardrobe. I feel a slight sensation of itching.

The voice continues. Strange verdicts, ancient punishments, are offered from the same booming resonance. To the snake, who now slithers. To the woman: promised future pain. The loud voice seems both sad and angry, even disappointed. But what the hell did I do?

Something about a certain tree. Susan has warned me about my unfiltered impudence. It didn't seem to help matters when I say, "Look, sir, if you didn't want us to touch the tree, why'd you plant the damn thing here in the first place?"

The voice doesn't find this funny. I'll have to pull weeds out of the garden from now on and sweat while doing so, but this is not much different from the life I have now. I shrug my shoulders.

More anger. "AND TO DUST YOU SHALL RETURN!"

Thank the Lord. A Lutheran voice after all! Grace is out there somewhere on the future horizon.

Baptists don't observe Ash Wednesday.

2:54 PM

Exactly fifteen minutes since totality's conclusion. But it sure seems like a lot longer.

I'll be forever grateful to Carl, my good friend who drives Bus Eight for the school district. He honked several times a couple minutes ago, apparently, and just called me on the cell phone I'd placed in the back pocket of my gym shorts.

"Good Lord, Reverend! It's a good thing I had no students on my bus. I'm heading back up to the school after totality and see you standing buck naked in your front yard, gesturing at the sky. Are you okay? Everything all right on the home front, old bean?" Carl laughed over the phone but I could tell he sounded concerned.

"Yeah, yeah, you know. I was telling you the other day about my bike ride but I decided to dial back the plan and limit my ass-baring to our garden. Guess I lost track of the time."

"I'd say you did, Rev! You tell Susan, that excellent wife of yours, hello for me. But hey, never mind. I'll see her in a few over at the high school. She's got bus duty on Mondays, right?"

5:37 PM

Susan did not look all that happy as she turned up our driveway and exited the car, loaded down with several book bags. I was sitting on the porch with two glasses of wine (one for her) and the rest of the bottle iced in a portable cooler nearby. The afternoon had cooled off considerably. But she looked pretty hot, in more ways than one.

Cicadas hummed in the trees across the road, back to their normal volume. I chose not to return Susan's hard stare from the end of the sidewalk and instead pretended to notice an interesting bird flying across the pines towards the middle school.

"Carl told me all about your little encounter with totality. What in *the world* were you thinking?"

"I didn't break my promise! No bicycle! But something happened!"

She sat her book bags down on the porch, plopped down in the other rocker, and reached for the glass.

"So, tell me. What caused you to be standing in our front yard, in broad daylight, as naked as Adam?"

"Well, it wasn't quite broad daylight. But the story does indeed involve this broad."

Susan hated the word. "Oh, great, even better."

"You know the story from Genesis, right? The tree, the snake, fig leaves—all that?"

"Of course." Susan took another sip of wine and was starting to look even more worried.

"I know you're not going to believe this, but when the light returned to our yard, none of the familiar stuff was there. There was a woman, a stunningly beautiful woman, and we were both in trouble with this loud voice."

"And that woman was me in this vision you had, right? Or maybe a younger version of me?"

"Yes, exactly. She was you, from head to toe. Naked."

"And what did you do with her? Me?"

"I admired you. And that was all."

"All?"

"Well, we each received certain punishments. Just like in the story. And then my cell phone rang. I heard it back in the garage. Carl says he saw me standing in the garden and I have absolutely no explanation except to say I'm sorry and know that could have made things embarrassing for you at school. I called Carl back and asked him not to mention this to anybody but I guess he felt the need to tell you."

"I suppose it's every man's dream to be naked in the garden all day with Eve. Happy retirement," said Susan. "What can I expect next from you?"

"But what was that all about, really? A sign of some sort? A bit different than the apocalyptic fears of all the Left Behinders around here, wouldn't you say?"

"Maybe it's a clear warning to keep your frickin' clothes on while you're outside from now on."

I let her words sink in and then said, "I notice you didn't rule out the inside."

8:15 PM

What a strange day. Susan's inside watching some British television show about an Anglican minister who helps solve local crimes with his private investigator pal.

Walking in front of the television on the way to the bathroom, it seemed like a pretty good time to restate my case. "That pastor you're watching encounters some rather weird stuff, right?"

Susan sighs. "Yes, he does."

I return to my rocker on the front porch. Most of the birds have quieted. The long call of a Chuck Will's Widow sounds in measured throaty repetition from the woods across the street. I'm glad I'm not widowed, but do believe Susan when she says that my strange behaviors may send her "to an early grave."

Our neighbors, Red and Lynn, out for an evening walk, smile and wave. Red is actually grinning at me through the front yard trees as if sending some sort of cloaked message. I wave back.

The ancient Celts believed that a brief transparent intersection could occur between different periods of history, prompted by unusual meteorological events like an eclipse. In Scottish literature, natural springs of water are sites especially prone to historic disturbance.

Susan said inside just now that maybe I need to cut back on the afternoon consumption of gin and tonics, but it's worth noting, for the record, that our garden in the lower half of the yard is very close to an old wet-weather spring. Just sayin', as they say.

Over the tops of the trees toward the middle school, the last light of a beautiful evening plays tag with the pinks and purples of low cirrus clouds, my favorite form of sunset. The cicadas, quiet for the last half hour, rise in voice as a choir.

For just a moment, their sounds seem like words.

Holy, holy, holy.

11.

Never Underestimate

LINDSEY LEANS BACK IN his wooden swivel chair at the law office of "Solomon and Son PLLC" and smiles like a wise old tabby cat ingesting a field mouse after a long morning of pleasurable pursuit. The chair makes a slow and quiet creak as the rotund attorney repositions his wide posterior and gazes out the window down North Main Street at a blossoming Bradford pear tree and a young couple strolling their baby along the ludicrously narrow sidewalk that will finally be widened this spring, after a long and heated debate concerning the wisdom of county tax hikes.

The chair was also his dad's, an esteemed attorney in Solomon County who started the firm in 1938 after graduating summa cum laude from law school in Chapel Hill. Lindsey will be buried somehow with this piece of family furniture, offering opportunity to swivel in his spacious casket and still offer nuggets of wisdom from the grave.

I can tell he's about to offer some witty profundity, always allowing a good bit of silence to serve as dramatic précis, something he's known for in court and that absolutely infuriates the district judge (a longtime friend of the Solomons), who's started to time the pauses before calling counsel back to the task at hand. Lindsey sips some hot coffee I just delivered. The chair creaks again. More silence. I'm always content to wait him out and often wish it was this quiet in our sanctuary on Sundays before church starts with the noisy bunch I'm called to lead.

"Never underestimate the power of the pussy," he says towards the pear tree. Except the words come out as *nevah* and *powah* in the delightful South Carolina brogue I'll never tire of hearing. Lindsey swivels the chair away from the window and faces me. Our eyes meet. I've come to understand that listening is my main function in our friendship.

Lindsey and I have been meeting for seven years now, every Thursday at 11:00 AM, for prayer and sometimes a quick Bible study from the book of Genesis, that timeless saga of an extended family whose wantonly creative dysfunction over several generations undoubtedly gave birth to the practice and profession of the law. Everything from fratricide (chapter 4) to fornicating with your father-in-law while masquerading as a prostitute (chapter 38) to fleeing from the unwanted advances of your boss's wife (chapter 39) are all right there in the Bible's opening pages. We've rarely gotten much further.

Sometimes God is on trial during our Thursday morning conversations, for creating a world where so much stupidity seems to hold sway. Lindsey's long-time secretary, Wanda Jo, has been firmly instructed to "*nevah* interrupt my meeting with the *pastuh* except in case of a *diyah emuhgency.*"

Only once has Wanda Jo had to override the executive order: the Thursday morning Lindsey's wife dropped dead of a massive heart attack completely out of the blue, two years ago in late July. My teenage son, Josh, was mowing the Solomon's lawn and went in to get a glass of water. Lindsey's Buick beat the ambulance to his house. I led prayer right on the freshly mopped kitchen floor, both of us kneeling and crying over her warm body, my slacks sliding around on the new wax.

It wasn't the first time that sudden death birthed a close relationship with one of my parishioners. Our Thursday meetings took an even deeper turn. Lindsey, sworn to keep secrets in his profession, adopted me as the son he never had, a confidante to replace the open ears (and impressively discreet mouth) of his dead wife who'd served an important role in a small town filled with gossips.

"You know that couple who sit *neeyah* the stained-glass window with Jesus sweatin' drops of blood in the *gahden* of Gethsemane and seem as shy as a couple of Carolina chickadees?" I assure Lindsey that I do indeed know them, Brenda and Ralph Lorick. "Well, it seems that she's been screwin' the *plumbah* who's been inspecting her ample pipes with a frequency that would put any honest Roto-*Rootah* man to complete shame."

The news hardly surprised me, but I didn't tell Lindsey. Josh not only mows lawns but also is quite the impressive fix-it guy for someone who's only a teenager; surprising skills he did not inherit from his father. Josh was repairing some cracked dry wall in the Lorick's master bedroom last summer. He came home from working at their house and was playing one-on-one with his friend, Stephen, in the driveway under the lights. Through an open window in our upstairs den, I heard them talking down below. "You wouldn't believe all the gadgets I saw under their bed. I didn't even know what they all were for! Belts, blindfolds, handcuffs, a nurse's outfit, a cheerleader's uniform, a long rubber thing, the family Bible, and a bikini featuring the Stars and Bars. I probably shouldn't have been looking at all that stuff, but it was practically spilling out from under the bed like they wanted me to see it."

It didn't happen very often, but for once it appeared I knew more than Lindsey about a scandal in town.

*

From looking at his 1963 high school yearbook, *The Pine Bough*, you'd never have concluded that Lindsey would become the most highly regarded defense attorney in the upper half of the state. The Solomon surname did not convey wisdom in Lindsey's class picture, which seemed to reveal a confused and frightened teenager whose only school involvement outside the classroom was a season of JV golf in the spring of his sophomore year.

"An *entuhprise* I gave up after my playin' *pahdnah* brained an in-flight *malluhd* with a skulled pitchin' wedge on his approach shot to the elevated ninth green *ovah* at the *Rivah* and Racquet. The Sierra Club—those *absuhd* ecology idgets—tried to sue his family *ovah* a deceased *buhd* that was apparently *rayah* in *owah* neck of the woods. My legal life, *Pastuh*, was *bowan* with a wicked wedge shot."

Retiring from golf at age fifteen, all of Lindsey's spare time outside his studies was devoted to absorbing the intricacies of his daddy's law office. He swept up dust bunnies, polished the wood floors, took out the garbage, and eavesdropped on a colorful cast of county characters who poured out their strange and exotic stories to his father. Lindsey became skilled at an early age in reading people and sifting through discarded minutia. Brenda Lorick indeed knew exactly who to contact when her husband filed for divorce and full custody of their three children "on grounds of unfaithfulness and flamboyant harlotry."

*

I have to admit that it took a lot of guts and courage to sing in the choir that Sunday. The news of her infidelity was all over town and I noticed every alto on the second row gave Brenda a wide berth in the balcony loft. I also observed even more craned necks looking back and up at the tense choral seating arrangement than when little Daisy Mae Sutherland, our fourteen-year-old musical prodigy, brought the entire congregation to tears last Christmas Eve with her moving rendition of Ave Maria.

Brenda was in the balcony with the choir. Ralph, her wounded and riled husband, was in the third row surrounded by seven protective and chatty widows, and Lindsey sat in the back pew, his customary Sunday morning post, taking it all in with chained reading glasses perched on the end of his nose. Before communion, even upon emphasizing *"for the forgiveness of sins"* with more volume than usual in the Eucharistic prayer, I could feel several pairs of eyes daring me to actually offer the bread and wine to everyone present.

Lutherans are all about grace, but with sensible limits. And Brenda, if a vote were taken, did not qualify for admittance at the Lord's Table in the hearts and minds of most. When I pressed the communion wafer into her shaky palm, an entire row of altar guild volunteers left the service early with no one to clean up afterwards. Washing the little glasses made me late for lunch at home but also offered a quiet moment to reflect upon my meeting with Lindsey next Thursday.

*

I'm still not sure whether confidential revelations with an attorney would pass muster with a synodical ethics committee. I tell Lindsey almost everything (knowing he'd never repeat it) and he tells me a lot, especially about his clients who are also my parishioners. You need somebody to talk to in professions like ours, or the burden of it all will eat you alive over time, from the inside out. Lindsey is quite astute theologically and helps me see Bible connections (even outside Genesis) I'd never before considered.

He became my bishop in many ways since the real guy is three hours away (minimum) at the state capital. With his wife gone and mine involved with various guilds and her own set of church friends (and my insistence that she have a life in town apart from her husband), Lindsey and I share

Thursday morning information that absolutely has to stay in his office. If someone bugged our conversations, he'd be disbarred and I'd be defrocked. "To be *disbahed* in Solomon County would make my daddy blush all the way from the *graveyahd*, and to be defrocked just sounds plain *duhty*, like the *pastuh's* willy needs an *emuhgency* dose of *Viagrah*." I've never repeated that line to anyone but it makes me laugh every time I think about it.

*

Brenda Lorick grew up on the western edge of the county on a bluff high above the Chattooga River with chickens, a patch of corn, seven dogs, and a mom who somehow scraped up enough money each week to feed her Hydrocodone habit. (I learned that little tidbit from Lindsey, who's gotten the mother out of jail more than once.) It was widely known that Brenda's father, Paul, beat the hell out of her and the two sisters for even looking at a boy.

The family came to our church occasionally, mostly on Wednesday nights for the weekly covered-dish supper, until I kept getting complaints that Brenda's father would always barge through first in line and clean out half the potato salad before anyone else got a chance to eat. The Senior Saints, our older ladies' circle who'd labored all afternoon, were livid at such a coarse paucity of manners. "Either you tell that hog to slow down or we will." I had a word with Paul. He didn't like it and his family never returned.

The county DSS more than once took the girls away, but they always found their way back to the wretched house on the river after the leg welts had time to heal. "The Social *Suhvices* needs a good swift ball peen *hammuh dye-rected* at *thayah* collective empty noggins," Lindsey offered one Thursday morning.

I was glad when Brenda and Ralph showed up in my office six Octobers ago and told me their plans. They were only eighteen, but I married them on the spot and offered to pay their gas to Gatlinburg just to get Brenda away from her family as fast as possible. When they returned from the honeymoon, the young couple joined our church and the three babies came one right after the other. I baptized each one of them in successive years on the Sunday after Easter, when the story of Doubting Thomas is usually read.

After his drywall repair job, Josh did find enough sex toys under Brenda and Ralph's bed to make a person think they owned stock in the Exit

100 Adult Fantasy Store over on I-85 near Spartanburg. There's a dark part of me that wants to go in that place myself to prowl around, but Lindsey's law voice always interrupts my imagination as the fantasy turns nightmarish and I run into parishioners purchasing naughty lingerie on aisle three: "*Pastuh*, what *wuh* you thinking?"

Even though Josh got a teenage eyeful that afternoon, and even though "the *plumbah*" was eventually involved with Brenda whose aforementioned "*powah*" is indeed formidable, it's not what you think. This situation fooled me. It even fooled Lindsey.

*

There's a story in the Bible where a woman meets Jesus at high noon at the town well. They talk awhile alone right out in public, which was scandalous enough at the time, and then Jesus with his x-ray eyes asks to meet the woman's husband, knowing full well she's had five and isn't married to her current live-in. This exposure of her past seems to liberate the woman, who is grateful beyond all get-out that someone finally knows about all the mistakes and darkness, but accepts her fully anyway. She traipses all over town inviting shocked residents to "Come and see this guy who told me everything I've ever done!" She's unexpectedly and deliriously happy, but I suspect that rather racy invitation raised a few eyebrows in the neighborhood.

Brenda wanted us both there for the Friday afternoon meeting at the law office—her attorney and her pastor. Even though we regularly shared "*puhtinent*" information with each other over the years, this was a first for each of us. But Brenda was insistent. She wanted to tell this only once to two men she trusted. It all came out quickly. Her husband had never desired her; the children were a cover for Ralph's true sexual preferences; and all the toys under the bed "were my foolish attempts to get somebody to finally love me."

She broke down and cried for thirty minutes, blubbering out her story. When Brenda left, Lindsey admitted he was wrong about the source, but refused to retract the word in future conversations describing her. "She's possibly the most *powahful* woman I've *evah* known. I've completely *undah*-estimated her."

*

When my brothers and I were very young, unbeknownst to my father, my mother left us with a babysitter and drove to a downtown Chattanooga courtroom to witness the sordid divorce proceedings of a crumbling marriage in our neighborhood. My mother wasn't alone. A dozen female friends were also present. A cuckolded husband was granted justice that day. On the way out, the fallen wife noticed my mom and her cohorts in the gallery. "I hope you all burn in hell," she told them. My mother remembers laughing.

The Solomon County courthouse was built just after the Civil War by emancipated slaves of Lindsey's ancestors. Not much has changed with the exterior of the building since then; ditto with the interior of many citizens whose lives are primarily defined by the borders of a small town. A salacious divorce draws a large crowd for people with not much else to do. We're still the state's only county (a law dating to 1902) with judge, jury, and public access for acrimonious family court trials.

Lindsey dressed impeccably, but was always especially coiffed to the nines for court. He wore a purple handkerchief in his coat pocket whenever appearing before a judge. I asked him once about this style choice. "I want to impress upon the ladies and gentlemen of the *joory* that it seems to be *forevah* like Lent around *heeyah*." I couldn't argue with him there.

Here's the strange thing that came out in the court proceedings, unearthed somehow by Lindsey's rabid research habits. Turns out that Ralph Lorick is not only gay but also the closeted statewide chair of the South Carolina Secessionist Party, whose main mission is the attempt to reinstall removed Confederate flags at public monuments across the state, explaining, I suppose, Brenda's bikini choice. Lindsey predicts that Ralph's fellow secessionists will not be all that excited upon learning of their leader's sexuality.

My favorite quote from the morning paper: "Respected attorney Lindsey Solomon asserted, 'I envision a border war between two competing seceding sub-states: Gayfederate South Carolina and Hetero-Confedero South Carolina. Ironically, they might go to battle under the very same flag.'" The reporter, of course, could not include voice inflection in his article. But I clearly heard "bowdah warwah."

*

Well, thank God some of the town heat has now been deflected away from Brenda Lorick. Poor thing. Her little fling seems mild now in retrospect. The altos have even welcomed her warmly back to the choir loft. She'll recover. I've just scheduled a wedding for Brenda and her paramour the plumber and feel certain there's enough shit to be unstopped in Solomon County in coming years to keep Brenda's three children dressed smartly for school for many autumns to come.

Last Thursday morning, I told Lindsey about all the wedding plans. He called Brenda's lover-plumber her "*powah mowah*." Power mower? Took me a moment to translate that one, even though I'd just handed it to him.

1 2 .

Blameless

HE's ALWAYS HAD THIS routine. Arriving early in the morning dark, Venus still visible on the eastern horizon, the chaplain parks his aging Corolla in the reserved space opposite the fence topped with coiled razor wire, pulls on his running shoes, and slips the dress loafers into his briefcase. Before placing the ID pendant around his neck, he glances at the picture dangling from the rearview mirror. Hard to believe it's been fifteen years since he first walked into this place fresh out of seminary, nervous and full of fear, like a deer in a hundred glaring headlights.

Wanda Jenkins, the policewoman at the main entrance with more years of experience than anyone on the prison staff, pats him down. She pushes the conveyor belt button and places the briefcase on the moving surface. "Does Miss Cindy ever get suspicious about the places where a black woman has to feel you up, Reverend?"

Simon Lassiter laughs at his friend. "We'd create quite the stir if we ran away together, Wanda. I think you'd get tired of a spoiled younger white man and I'm not sure the inmate population here at Southern state prison would ever get over it. Cindy did want me to ask about your momma. How she's doing?"

"Lawd, help my time. Please keep prayin' for her, Rev. The doc says the stroke will leave her left side permanently paralyzed, Jehovah bless her sassy soul. That woman's still right bossy yet fo' all her many afflictions. So, pray for me, too. Send up a few on my behalf so I don't slap ole momma silly."

Simon again laughs. "Your whole family's in my prayers, Wanda. I promise." He retrieves his briefcase on the far side of the scanner and makes his way through two additional checkpoints and doors whose pass codes even a chaplain is not privy to. The echoing clang as the doors close behind him always reminds Simon of the age of this ancient South Carolina low country structure, the sounds traveling back in time to reveal so many faces—cocky, depressed, angry, a few truly repentant—lingering down the long hallway that leads to his office. Some have made it out successfully, safely. He knows the difficult reality of his job with men he's come to love: most don't.

*

The old track circling the prison exercise field is quiet as Simon runs laps. Weeds and grass sprout through the cracks in the oval surface. A barred owl flies low and silent over the field, looking larger in the near-dark, and roosts in the far stand of trees alongside the river that serves as the prison's natural eastern boundary.

Old stories still circulate about escapees who used the river to mask their short-lived flight from captivity, often into a sultry climate more sweltering than the prison itself. A favorite involves an inmate who somehow managed to slip away undetected and dive from the top of the high stone border wall into a deep river pool at flood stage. His body was never recovered, the only resident who truly managed to escape the place—a certain drowning. Many still maintain he could hold his breath as long as Houdini and is out there somewhere, on the lam, like that guy in *The Shawshank Redemption*.

A dog barks several times from the large dairy farm on the opposite side of the river and then settles. Incidents occur that disrupt the daily prison schedule, including an early morning riot several years ago where Simon served as lead negotiator between inmates and correctional officers. Cindy wanted him to quit and "find a normal church" after the riot. It made the national news and the high school principal had to call Ms. Lassiter out of class to report what was happening with her husband.

But such incidents are rare. Cindy doesn't worry very much about her husband anymore. "We love chaplains in here," an inmate named Josh once told Simon. "If anybody was ever dumb enough to hurt you, that poor sumbitch wouldn't live through the night." The chaplain always found this statement strangely comforting.

The same is usually true for Cindy after years of watching her husband head off to work in such a place, but a primary reason they've never had children is her fear that they might turn out like some of the men Simon describes. In some ways, the prison population has become a proxy family for the couple. A significant portion of their income anonymously funds various canteen supplies, especially at Christmas, for men whose relatives have largely given up on them.

As he runs, Simon thinks how the prison is even calmer at this hour than his own neighborhood. It's a good time to pray. Images of various men and their unique challenges find intersection with his measured breath and steady footfalls around the track. He likes running in circles rather than linearly. It's one of the few things in any day he can measure accurately with documented progress.

Although Chaplain Lassiter hasn't believed in the literal interpretations of many Bible stories since his childhood in a Lutheran church, and certainly doesn't buy that a woman and man were occupants of an unsullied garden somewhere in Asia many millennia ago, he does appreciate the theological concept of limits and boundaries and how unbidden consequence will always shadow particular infraction like night following day.

The inmates who attend Simon's daily Bible study like to revisit Eden and the Genesis fallout with fervent regularity. "Those cats were warned!" thundered Zeke Smith, a lifer with no hope of parole, the previous afternoon. "It's not like those two assholes had the wrong information and were tricked by some sneaky snake. Don't go blamin' no rascally reptile. They knew the rules. So did I. Nobody to blame here but me. Ain't that the way of it, Rev?"

Simon often believes those inside a prison accept blame at some point a lot better than many on the outside who are always projecting fault onto somebody else. There's always plenty of blame to go around and reflect upon in prison life. A chaplain's work is largely about what's next after accepting responsibility for what brought them there, even though such acceptance also involves the probability of never leaving.

*

Following his early morning run and a shower—the private bathroom an enticement by the warden to keep a good chaplain around as long as possible—Simon looks over a stack of messages. Most are clearance requests for inmates who need to be transported by police officers to funerals of immediate family, usually a parent, in various corners of the state. The chaplain is often called upon to weigh in on whether attendance at a funeral would be helpful or detrimental for all concerned.

An inmate known as Shorty by everyone at Southern Correctional pokes just his head—sporting a crew cut and rather mischievous dark eyes—around the open doorway. "Hey, Rev Simon, you got a minute?"

Simon knows this encounter will take longer than a minute. He pushes several boxes of donated Bibles to the back wall of the office and makes room for the little man in one of the folding chairs. Simon has often made a mental note to learn Shorty's real name. This time he sketches a tiny stick figure on a sticky note, quickly affixing the orange adhesive square to a lower cabinet behind his desk where he'll be sure to see it.

A trusty in the prison, Shorty couldn't go just anywhere, but did seem to have more freedom of range than most—especially remarkable for a man who occasionally remembers, pretty much out of the blue, where in the state he buried one of his murder victims, numbering now in the dozens.

Earlier in the year, Shorty woke up one morning and reported the following to a correctional officer: "Highway 700 in Colleton County. Turn left at a T-stop and then a quick right down a forest service road. Leave your car at the old fire tower, cross a small creek, and walk about fifty paces towards the setting sun. Look for an old loblolly pine tree, the biggest one around if it's still there. Dig at the base closest to the creek." This information led to the remains of a body, a young girl, whose case had been cold for at least twenty years.

Perhaps the most notorious serial killer in South Carolina history and a beneficiary of the state moratorium on the death penalty, Shorty was a model prisoner since his incarceration, whose sporadic memory and good behavior earned him a few privileges, including the freedom to peek into Chaplain Simon Lassiter's office pretty much whenever he felt like it. Simon always thought the little man seemed like the most unlikely and affable murderer you'd ever want to meet—short in stature, yes, but incredibly long-winded and friendly.

This would indeed take good bit longer than a minute.

The next morning, the same owl (or a close cousin) flew low over the exercise field and perched near the river. Must be after field mice or chipmunks, maybe a squirrel, Simon thinks. Grateful for air that's certainly cooler than any other part of the day, Simon also knows the heavy humidity in South Carolina in late summer never takes a rest.

The chaplain eases into a steady pace with a consistent heart rate after the third lap. His cotton T-shirt is already almost wet enough to obscure the dark university logo of a fighting gamecock, a shirt he wears occasionally to pacify the rabid football preferences of certain inmates, even though Simon attended Clemson as a psychology major.

As on other mornings, he prays for various men in particularly challenging situations and recalls how much of the New Testament was written by a certain inmate named Paul, whose jail record, if they thought about it, would still raise more than one eyebrow among normal church parishioners he knows on the outside.

Shorty's questions from their lengthy meeting yesterday still intrigued him. Simon had heard them before, of course, in his fifteen years at Southern; he was mostly interested in the questioner and the origins of his concerns.

"I been readin' about the commandments in the Old Testament, Rev. And I'm pretty sure there's not a single one I haven't broken. God knows exactly who he's dealin' with when I send up prayers to the Big Guy in the Sky. You with me? You follow me?"

Simon hated this pair of questions, partly because his own father used them with a certain frequency that made Simon crazy as a teenager. He almost told Shorty, sarcastically, that no, he didn't understand how a serial killer with state-wide notoriety had managed to break so many rules and could he be specific about exactly which commandments his history of infractions indeed covered.

"Yes," Simon had instead replied. "I'm right with you."

"Well, I skipped on over to the New Testament, where God and Jesus are a little softer on homeboys like me. And it was him saying *Do this* that really got my attention. You know, he didn't say think about doin' it. So, let me get this straight. You, as one of them certified forgivers, hand me a little bread and a sip of wine and I'm good and all cleaned up. Is that about the lowdown of it?"

"Well, we can't use wine in here. You know that, Shorty."

"But it says to use wine. Will it work without wine? Wouldn't the grape juice substitute be a little like usin' a gun with blanks? I had a friend, ex-friend, who set me up once in a bank holdup with a gun loaded with fake bullets. We got away, but holy shit and ha-ha and all that. I had to kill him. Strangled him in his sleep. He's one of the people I dumped down an abandoned well over in Florence County. But he really shouldn't count in my murder total because I was doin' God a favor by riddin' the world of that scumbag. You with me?"

Remembering yesterday's conversation with Shorty, Simon laughed out loud on lap five at the absurdity of the amended body count. He wondered sometimes what this strange job was doing to him.

He also recalled a service with Holy Communion from several years ago when a prisoner ran a little business out of his cell with a fermented grape juice concoction he was tending in the water tank of his toilet. The guy had cleverly retained the juice in the back of his throat without swallowing and let time and an orange peel work their magic. A rather putrid hooch, but quite popular in the Wando Block. Simon had to get special clearance from the warden to distribute Christ's body and blood after that incident.

*

Forty men, including Shorty, packed the small chapel one Sunday morning a few weeks later. Sometimes a local Lutheran congregation received approval to bring music and even a few cut flowers from the garden of a church member. An old donated piano, out of tune but serviceable, was tightly wedged into the corner, regularly played by a diminutive man named Fred whose long nose and disheveled hair gave him the odd appearance of a musical Ichabod Crane. The men loved him, especially when Fred stopped a badly paced hymn in mid-verse and shouted, "Okay, work with me, people!"

Simon's sermon style for a prison setting was conversational rather than overly prepared. He pretty much knew what direction he'd like the message to take, but allowed interruptions and commentary from the inmates, who were encouraged to toss out questions at any time. Simon was used to colorful queries mid-sermon and could often tell the men had been thinking about the Sunday morning Bible text that he would post on his office door ahead of time each Friday morning.

The opening hymn died down. Fred rose from the piano bench to commend the men for singing "In Christ There is No East or West" with such fervent gusto. Simon made a few announcements, including a prayer request from a man named Jack who was absent that morning, in route with police escort to his mother's funeral service in McClellanville. When anyone's parent died in the prison, especially somebody's momma, the men who attended chapel all signed a card Simon would bring.

Simon also noted that the men would be celebrating Holy Communion that morning with special permission from the warden. A couple men in the back laughed. Simon also smiled but said, "I think everyone in this room knows that this will be the last time we celebrate communion here at Southern Pen Chapel if a certain historic incident repeats itself." The entire room turned around to look at the two men who'd laughed.

After a second hymn about the wideness of God's mercy, the chaplain read the account of the Last Supper according to Saint Luke. "Don't miss this," Simon said. "In the night when Judas betrayed Jesus to the authorities for thirty pieces of silver, he ate dinner with that very guy, knowing full well what the betrayer was about to do! It's almost like he forgave the guy ahead of time! What do you guys make of this?"

Shorty stood up. A collective groan rose in pitch from all assembled. "Let the man speak," said Simon.

"Look, everyone here knows my record. I'm pretty sure I've screwed up more times than anybody in this room. But let me get this straight, Rev. You're gonna give each of us a taste and a sip and say a few holy words. And that's it? We're all forgiven? Clean starts, all that. I like that idea, but Jesus H. Christ, it hardly seems fair. Almost too good to be true. Y'all with me? Follow me?"

The men all nodded in recognition of a deal that did indeed seem pretty crazy. Shorty continued. He looked almost angry.

"Where does the blame go, Rev? Somebody's got to pay, right? Does one man just somehow soak up everybody's screw-ups and we move on squeaky-clean, free as birds until we fuck up again? Can anybody be forgiven with a tiny taste? What about somebody like Hitler? What about somebody like me?"

A large man named Bobby, tattooed with coiled snakes on his arms, spoke up. "God told me you in particular will fry in hell, Shorty, you little shit. Sit down and shut up. Let's hear what the Rev has to say."

Simon was quiet for a few moments. He'd been asked these questions before. The men admired him, trusted him. They looked up at their chaplain in a way that reminded him of his old fourth grade teacher, Mrs. Henry, whose young pupils trusted her authority and guidance much like baby birds trust their mother. The word of God was like food for these men in a wilderness where all the roads had vanished. Simon wanted to get it right.

"A long time ago," he said, "a young man basically told his father to drop dead. The guy was probably about the age of many of you. He wanted his share of the inheritance even before his dad died. It was a crazy request, without honor for a parent, but the generous father gave his son the money anyway. Who knows exactly what that young man got into, but it wasn't very good. You follow me, Shorty?"

All the men laughed.

"One day the young man came to his senses. He had his speech all planned. Surely his dad would take him back if he acted sorry enough. And he was sorry. He'd work as his father's slave. He walked home. A long way home. You know what happened then?"

A quiet man on the front row who hardly ever spoke said almost in a whisper: "That daddy beat the hell out of his son."

"No, he didn't, even though the son probably deserved it." Simon made a mental note to talk to the quiet man later that week. "The father threw a party for his lost son. He was so glad to see him again. He invited the neighbors. He made some of the best hamburgers you've ever tasted from the steer that won the blue ribbon at the Columbia State Fair. And everybody danced and sang far into that evening because they were all so glad to see that young man again."

Shorty stood up again. "But you're forgettin' somethin', Rev. Not everybody was happy. That older brother was pretty hot about the party, am I right?"

"You're exactly right, Shorty. The older brother refused to attend. Why do you think that was?"

"Because that kid didn't deserve all that attention. He deserved a good ass-kickin'. That's what I'm sayin', Rev. Even with all I've done, all my own mistakes and ornery ways, I'm not sure I would a gone in and sung about it, even if old Fred had been playin' the pie-anner that day. Somebody's got to pay. Somebody's got to accept the blame. It doesn't seem fair that a tiny taste of bread and a sip of juice will wipe away everything we've all done.

It's a hell of an idea, but shit, Jesus is crazy as a loon to forgive somebody like me. It's like he runs a free-for-all with all the nut jobs of this old world."

Somebody from the back yelled out. "Sit down, Shorty! We don't want you at our party anyway."

Fred stood up and said he figured everyone knew "Amazing Grace" by heart. He played the song several times through as the men came forward in single file towards Simon for the bread and grape juice.

"For you . . . for you . . . for you," he repeated.

Many of the men were crying.

*

The next morning, a Monday, Simon decided to walk around the track instead of run. On the fourth lap, he heard someone from a window call his name from the near wall, almost inaudibly. In the dark, the chaplain couldn't detect the exact cell from which the voice called out. He walked through the tall wet grass, badly in need of mowing, and listened. The voice he heard seemed almost disguised, intentionally raspy, close to a whisper.

"Rev Simon, I couldn't give two shits about that little weasel, Shorty. He's got what's comin' to him, anything twisted some warped fucker in here might dream up. But I thought you should know, a man a God and all, that there's a rumor in the block grapevine that the little midget's about to receive his comeupper, or whatever the hell it's called. Today before noon."

Simon tried to walk toward the voice in order to locate the cell later. At least the tier. He crept closer to the wall. "Tell me how you know all this." Silence. He repeated the same words again, with more volume. Nothing.

Simon walked quickly to his office, skipped the shower, and phoned the warden at home. He also called the head correctional officer on Shorty's unit and asked for someone to escort the little man to the chaplain's office as soon after breakfast as possible.

The chaplain, shaken, knelt on the small prayer bench in the office corner that his grandfather, also a Lutheran pastor, had given him upon his ordination. Simon sometimes used the kneeler with individual prisoners wanting to confess something specific prior to the laying on of hands with anointing. The inscription in the wooden base was from the book of Colossians: "You have died, and your life is hidden with Christ in God."

"Lord," he began, "you died between two thieves and even asked forgiveness for your tormentors. You know Shorty's heart. Nobody much likes this guy. You've seen all he's done; far more than anybody here but you and this little man can really know. But I'm sure of your divine love for him despite all his flaws. Give insight and wisdom to another flawed servant kneeling here this morning. Something sinister is about to happen, something evil. Help me interrupt this planned darkness. Use me as an instrument of your peace."

After meeting with the warden to explain what he'd heard at the wall early that morning, Simon prayed with Shorty, who'd been reluctantly escorted to his office. He listened to the chaplain's concerns with a grinning smirk. "Aw hell, Rev. No worries. It's not the first time somebody's tried to kill me. I ain't skeered a nobody. Shit, I of all people know what death looks like. You tell anybody here they can come get me."

Though it felt a little like theology he really didn't believe as he made the offer, Simon asked if Shorty wanted to receive communion, privately, right then and there at the prayer bench. The little man laughed. "What? First you tell me the tiny taste and sappy sip will wash away even *my* dark sins. And now you're tellin' me the body and blood's gonna give me some magical cloak of protection against these big-bodied blood brothers here at Southern? No thanks, Rev. I'll take my chances."

Shorty was escorted back to his block by a different officer. Thirty minutes later, he turned on his cell radio and an explosion almost ripped his face off. It was later learned that someone on the outside wanted Shorty dead. And an ingenious bomb inside the radio, timed to ignite with the "on" switch, came close to doing the trick on the spot.

*

Shorty didn't wake up for two days. And when he did—there in the prison infirmary with compassionate nurses and a visiting physician—Simon was at his bedside, had just finished a prayer, and was now telling him a story.

"This rich guy ran a vineyard up in Oconee County where the soil was just right for eventual wine production from the grapes. One late summer he had a bumper crop but not enough grape pickers."

Shorty spoke. "Good Lord, Rev. Enough with the Bible."

"Silence, wee man," said the chaplain. He continued.

"The rich guy drove to the town square in downtown Walhalla five times all through the day—at dawn, nine, noon, three, and five. He piled any picker he could find into the bed of his pickup truck, dumped them out on his farm and said, 'Get to work.'"

"Hey, I know this one," said Shorty, whose head bandage needed changing and was oozing something strange that wasn't exactly blood.

"I'm glad. Listen. They tell me you're not supposed to be talking for a change. Are you with me? Follow me?"

Shorty smiled.

"So, the sun is setting at the end of the day," Simon said. "And all the grape pickers line up for their wages. But here's the crazy thing. The first guys in line, the ones who only worked an hour, looked in their pay envelopes and almost shit a brick."

"You're not 'sposed to be sayin' words like that, Rev."

"Well, get over it. Anyway, they looked at their cash and the crazy owner had given them a full day's pay. They couldn't believe it."

"And don't you bet those haughty suckers who'd been there since dawn were counting their chickens."

Simon laughed. "Yes, I'll bet they were. But you know what happened." Shorty nodded.

"They were all paid exactly the same, no matter how long they'd worked that day. What do you make of that story, Shorty?"

"I'd say the jackasses who sweated the most were a little pissed. Am I right, Rev?"

"Yeah, they were, Shorty."

"It's a little like that other nutty story you told us in the chapel the other Sunday, right? About the guy who thought his pissant little brother should get his ass switched until it bled instead of havin' some fuckin' party thrown on his bee-haff."

"It's a lot like that other story, Shorty. Jesus reveals to us a lot about how God works when he tells these stories."

Simon waited for a response, but Shorty had fallen back under a deep sleep from the pain relievers. The chaplain laid his hands lightly on the little man's head, said another prayer, and began to walk back to his office.

Just before he was coded out into the long hallway outside the infirmary, a nurse called Simon back.

Shorty, fighting sleep, asked the chaplain if he might bring him communion. "That body and blood voodoo you do," he said.

Wanda Jenkins was working the main entry checkpoint to the prison the following Sunday morning as Simon arrived early to prepare for the weekly chapel service. He didn't run on Sundays.

"I don't know how you keep comin' back here, Rev. I hardly ever leave my little post here at the front door, but I can imagine some of the horse crap (forgive me, Jesus) you have to put up with back there. I know you tried to be friends with that sorry little man but I'm not one bit sorry he died the other night. I know the Lord forgave even the people who killed him on the cross, but I sure ain't Jesus, if you haven't noticed."

Simon smiled at his friend. "And neither am I, Wanda. It's not the easiest thing to follow the man's instructions. Sometimes I read what he says in the Gospels and think it doesn't make a lick of sense. Words for another world maybe. A kingdom coming our way."

Wanda shook her head slowly, and then said with some volume. "Exactly what the man said to pray for! On this old earth, just as it sho' is promised up heavenly way."

"I heard somebody once say that God will receive anyone into heaven who can stand it."

"Well, if yo' man Shorty is there, I may not be able to. Stand it, that is."

Simon hugged Wanda and took his briefcase from the opposite side of the conveyor belt. His friend hugged him back, forgetting for a moment to pat him down. She was crying. Simon tried handing her a tissue he'd fished from a briefcase pocket.

"Get on back there with your people," she said.

*

Fred the pianist was playing Simon's favorite hymn, "Come Thou Fount of Every Blessing," as the men filed into the chapel for worship. They'd heard about Shorty and were unusually quiet as Simon rose to speak.

"Maybe you've also thought at times that about the only thing the little man had in common with Jesus was that they were both pretty much hated by almost everybody at the end of their lives. Shorty was a hard man to love. His real name was Andrew, by the way. I want you to know he loved you men. Last Friday, just before he died, he asked me to tell all of you that."

Simon left some silence, as he normally did, for anyone to speak. But no one did. The chapel was as quiet as a monastery.

"You may not know that Shorty grew up in pretty bleak poverty and hardly had a roof over his head. He was a difficult child—hard to raise, a little hellion even as a kid. In order to keep him from running away when he was just a little boy, even shorter than he is now, his momma sometimes pushed him down into a hole she'd dug in the backyard and filled the hole up to his neck with dirt, especially when she had to leave for a while. One time she didn't come back for two days."

Simon again left some silence.

"Shorty doesn't remember much about his daddy, who left when he was young, except that he drank a lot and hit them all the time. The father left the home for good and then nobody saw him anymore."

One of the men, Samuel, spoke so softly that Simon asked him to repeat it.

"I wonder why God, if he's good and all, lets people suffer that way." Several of the men nodded their heads.

Samuel continued. "What Shorty did to all those people, so many victims, had somethin' to do with how he was raised. Had to at least have caused a bit of the meanness. I'm here because of my own stupid fault. Had great parents, still do."

Simon allowed Samuel's question to hang in the air for a full minute. He finally spoke.

"Thank you for asking that question, Samuel. I really thank you for stating it so honestly. There are no easy answers to it and if some minister tries to offer you a quick answer then I'd run the other way as fast as possible. The Bible is full of people wondering about the nature of God and why God allows certain things to happen. And part of the answer (and we talked about this a bit when we studied Genesis last month) is the careful balance between our freedom and God's control. God allowing us to go our own way if we choose a wrong path, not because he doesn't love us but because he didn't want to create robots who always choose the right thing. If love, for example, is the only thing you could possibly choose, is that really love at all? But your question, Samuel, is even deeper than that I think, right? If God created a beautiful world with laws and choices and consequences way back when (consequences that sometimes result in a prison sentence), what specifically does God do for us now? Just watch when bad stuff happens to little kids like Shorty? Just watch when the little man did bad stuff, maybe as a result of bad things happening to him? Just watch when somebody rigs up a radio to get even, payback time?"

More silence filled the chapel. Simon continued. "We are wrestling with questions this morning that have no easy answers. But I need to tell you a story to give a bit of perspective to the question Samuel's asking. Keep thinking about his question while I tell it."

Fred accidentally leaned on several lower piano keys, creating a dissonant bong, which caused the men to laugh. They needed to laugh and all looked his way.

"Okay, so arrest me," said Fred, with feigned dramatic emphasis. "But also forgive me, for crying out loud. I've heard you men sing. If this were a chemistry lab, we'd have blown up the place a long time ago." More laughter.

Simon allowed the men to settle down. "I know you all remember how Shorty wouldn't take communion when we shared it here in chapel, saying it didn't seem fair to have all his sins wiped away with a bit of bread and a sip of juice. Last Thursday I took him communion over in the infirmary. He asked me to bring it. And if you think about it, a pretty appropriate day of the week to share communion, right? Same day so long ago that Jesus took off his robe and wrapped a towel around his waist—the symbol of a servant—to wash the feet of his disciples."

"Yeah," Fred piped up, emboldened. "And I hope he washed his hands before supper after washing their feet. Because if those twelve guys had feet as stinky as mine, he probably should have worn rubber gloves." The men howled at the pianist.

"Don't distract the preacher, Fred," said Simon. "But he does bring up a point. Washing feet was the height of grunt work. Slaves did it. The divine blameless one sent by God was stooping down to the very lowest level. And afterwards, right after a job worse than cleaning toilets, he invited everyone to a dinner that included the very guy who gave him away! I think this was what Shorty finally saw there at the end of his life. Communion isn't magic. Communion is God's way of saying that nobody should be left out. Jesus didn't just watch people suffer, Samuel. He didn't just observe. He got down in the suffering, so to speak. He entered their crap. He may not have been put down in a hole like Shorty, but he was sure strung up on a cross. Communion is a way of saying we're all in this together, full of questions, even doubt. Shorty wanted that sort of communion before he died. You were his family, more than you know."

As the men filed forward for the bread and grape juice later in the service, Fred played "Let Us Break Bread Together on Our Knees," a favorite among them.

They sang, "When I fall down on my knees, with my face to the rising sun, O Lord, have mercy on me." Simon was the one crying this time.

*

Early the next morning, on his eighth lap, Simon reached clarity about an opportunity recently posed by his bishop in Columbia. "There's an opening at a large congregation up in Greenville. I'd like for you to consider interviewing there. You've done marvelous work at Southern, but maybe the Spirit is calling you to a new sort of ministry. There's a county detention center not far from the church. You could still be involved in prison ministry in your spare time."

Simon was intrigued. Cindy would worry about him less; more money certainly, the prestige of a tall steeple.

He prayed through all seven laps, bringing each name and face of his little chapel flock to mind. He thought of Shorty's bandaged head and outstretched hands as he received communion for the first time in his life on the Thursday before he died last Friday.

But it wasn't until the eighth lap that he recalled a man he met on Death Row as a student chaplain in seminary, an inmate named Robert who was trying to decide whether to live or die. He'd given up and wanted to be executed in the state's electric chair for a crime he'd committed as a young man. A steady stream of ministers had visited the row, telling the men they were all bound for hell anyway. Robert's thinking had become pretty clear and straightforward: Why not go ahead and get it over with?

The same owl (at least the chaplain assumed so) flew low over the field as he thought of his encounter with Robert so many years ago, an inmate who'd changed his mind about dying after talking with Simon. They still wrote one another after all this time. Robert was even leading a Bible study with fellow prisoners these days.

The owl landed in the stand of trees near the river. Simon suddenly knew he needed to stay right where he was with men who needed him. And also, men he needed.

He finished his run, went inside to catch up on the latest news from Wanda's family, passed through the two checkpoints, and walked down the long hallway towards his office.

His favorite hymn came to mind and he hummed along with the words forming in his imagination. *Oh, to grace how great a debtor daily I'm constrained to be. Let that grace now like a fetter bind my wandering heart to thee.*

Simon removed his sweaty jogging clothes and stepped into the shower. As the water streamed over his body, he watched it pool for a moment at his feet, then disappear somewhere far below him.

13.

I Drive Your Truck

*If we had a keen vision and feeling of all ordinary human life, it
would be like hearing the grass grow and the squirrel's heart beat,
and we should die of that roar which lies on the other side of silence.*
—George Eliot, *Middlemarch*

IT'S A NICE THOUGHT from Eliot's wise and steady pen, but I wish George
was up on our roof with me right now. I'd make her stay long enough to
hear a certain roar.

It's quiet for a change this Saturday morning on our wooded street that
meanders down a ridge above Cove Creek and ends about a mile from here
at the high school. We bought the house four years ago, escaping the noise
of the city. A confession: I climbed up here under the guise of cleaning pine
needles out of our clogged gutters. But I'm really hiding from the Lowe's
delivery guy who's inside right now talking with my wife. He delivered a
new washer ten minutes ago (we put off the matching dryer) because I bent
the hell out of our old one with a crowbar, trying to pop the lid off for a
simple repair. What man wants to face the shame of such a blunder in front
of an appliance professional?

So, I'm up here undercover with the birds and here I shall remain
until the hoses are all connected and the uniformed man has explained
to Catherine the intricacies of the new spin cycle. I should really be down
there. I do all the laundry, after all. But I'm reclining noiselessly on the
south side of the roof, a hint of frost on the shingles, listening for the truck's
departure and observing the tapping of a pileated woodpecker as she bores

into a dead pine tree filled with carpenter ants that's about to fall onto our neighbor's property. Bore on, Woodrow.

I read the other day that woodpeckers have rather long tongues to snatch their wiggly prey. Recalling this avian talent gives me the shivers in the morning chill. Only God and Catherine know I'm up here, safe for now from her penetrating gaze. (Catherine's, not God's, I hope.) Her tongue is another thing entirely, sharpened with dazzling alacrity after thirty-five years of marriage to the likes of me, easily able to snatch her prey even from this height.

The Lowe's van finally backs out of the driveway, astonishingly quiet for a vehicle that large. I could descend now with male ego largely intact, but the sun is just peeking through the pines, melting the chill. I almost fall asleep in tandem with the tapping, but my neighbor's truck roars to life with a volume that could wake the dead.

*

I'll never understand the insane desire to make one's truck or motor-cycle even louder than when it leaves the assembly line. Why in the wide world would anyone intentionally create a noise capable of penetrating brick and drywall? I Googled the idiotic fad the other day and discovered the process involves removing the rubber (sound-deadening) exhaust pipe mounts and replacing them with metal mounts that makes the whole oper-ation vibrate and the resulting sound "to more loudly resonate." I'm frankly way past the need for the intensification of sound resonation in my life.

We don't require an alarm clock these mornings because dawn arrives at 4:15 AM every weekday with gurgling petro-thunder filling every crevice of the bedroom as Diamond Smoak, our thirty-something neighbor, roars off to work at the Maxfli factory, an odd golf-related vocation for a loud truck purist, if you ask me.

Last year, Diamond bought the house next door from a lovely young couple who never made a peep. On the move-in day, he asked to borrow an adjustable wrench to put together a bed for his young son, who visits every other weekend. He seemed nice enough at the time, sporting a Braves cap (my favorite team) and denim overalls with a Harley-Davidson logo ironed on the back. I offered to help him move the heavy furniture, but he said plenty of help was on the way. We haven't talked much with Diamond since then and the wrench is still at large, but we hear him now several times a day, voluminously so. On the weekends, his friends bring over their loud trucks for beer and engine tinkering as they all compare muffler revvings like a drunken pit crew, an ironic twist on sounds devoid of anything resembling a muffle.

As the local Lutheran pastor, I'm obviously familiar with all the commandments and realize these are not just divine suggestions, but it didn't take long to start shredding number eight via fantasies of jamming a large potato up Diamond's tailpipe or pouring a bag of sugar into his gas tank, diverting blame to a band of Catherine's warped and covetous teenage students, most of whom are not quite old enough to have a loud truck of their own. It wouldn't take much to fudge a bit and creatively avoid the warning about bearing false witness against the neighbor. One might argue that my fantasy could turn into a faithful witness authored by the very ire of God.

I asked Catherine to take a poll of her students the other day concerning truck noise escalation and one little upstart named Owen had the gumption to say, "Why, it's just personal pref-rence, Ms. Greenway. It ain't hurtin' nobody, is it?"

Two springs ago we had a late freeze-warning in upstate South Carolina. While covering our blueberry bushes with bed sheets featuring the face of a large chicken (our children fell peacefully asleep under these for many years), I heard Diamond tucking his precious truck into his garage for the night with a loud and noxious automotive fart. The two evening actions, berries versus blather, along with the "Make America Great Again" sticker affixed to his quivering bumper, nicely underscored our household differences. Indeed, our neighbor was not hurting anybody with his personal preference, but he was beginning to significantly alter my blood pressure.

I've always been pastorally amused by the tension inherent in two of our favorite national slogans. "It's a free country," coupled with: "There ought to be a law against that." Since Eden's dawn, there's never been a satisfying balance drawn by those in moral authority between the gift of freedom and the necessity of limits and prohibition. Even though I wanted to smack young Owen upon hearing his rationale, I promised Catherine that we'd take the high road and handle this like reasonable Christians. It wasn't the first promise to her that I'd eventually break.

*

Not long after we moved here, I attended the funeral service for the father of one of our church members. I hadn't had a chance to meet her dad, but figured Mary needed some support from the church that morning. The family processed into the funeral home chapel to the opening lines of the deceased's favorite country-western song. Lutherans are not used to hearing words such as "89 Cents in the Ashtray" serving as the musical prelude in ritual solemnities, a rather jarring contrast to J. S. Bach.

Mary tried to catch my eye and gauge her pastor's reaction as the processional grazed my pew, but I pretended to look at the dual large screens up front, scrolling dozens of pictures of her dad sitting behind the wheel of his deep ocean blue metallic Chevy Silverado. The singer assured gathered mourners that he still drove the truck of his dead brother despite its horrible fuel efficiency. I fleetingly wondered what kind of truck Jesus might drive. He invites us in the Gospel of Luke to consider the lilies but I considered tires during the service instead, privately grateful to Mary's dad for helping me remember that the two on the front of my aging Toyota Corolla were almost entirely bald.

After the service, on the way to the hospital to check on a parishioner recovering from gall bladder surgery, I phoned Anna (our church secretary) and asked if she could make an afternoon appointment for me at Main Street Tire and Brake. I've always been rather fond of what Leroy, the proprietor, told her: "Yeah, I can git to it might near lunch atter I've had my three beers and made love to Susan." Susan, Leroy's wife, usually works in the front office. I never saw Susan that afternoon but can attest that I got a great deal on two new tires with a fairly decent 35K guarantee.

*

The transition for us from a large city church to a much smaller congregation in a tiny town upstate was largely driven, as I've mentioned, by a need to flee the relentless noise of urban sprawl and the interstate traffic jams every afternoon at five, which were beginning to wear on my pastoral nerves. One of my church members, a tightly wound man who served on the finance board, was once held overnight at the County Detention Center for getting into a fistfight with another motorist who cut him off at a tricky merger with a blaring horn and certain middle finger. When the line of cars came to a stop, they rolled around in the grassy median trading punches until the police arrived.

After ten years in the city, I told the bishop I'd be open to a quiet call with a less frenetic pace. Retirement was not that far off for either of us. The kids were all grown and gone. Catherine's been following me around the southeast, saint-like, through four parishes now in thirty-five years, her career usually taking a backseat to mine. I promised this would be the last move.

But Diamond Smoak has changed all that.

I've noticed in my work how the devil is rarely obvious. The temptations during those forty days in the wilderness, after all, do not look so bad to me from a distance. Stones to bread when famished. Gathering a following with a daring swan dive from a great height a la Johnny Weissmuller. Inheriting vast wealth that might fuel the fledgling movement. Well, sign me up. These temptations couldn't have looked all that bad to Jesus. Nothing obviously evil out there that might alert the Holy Spirit Police, right? After his famous test, I suspect Jesus may have concluded that the devil chooses to dress in drag.

A truck—even one that gurgles noisily like a loud Linda Blair releasing a vile torrent of vomit from the bowels of hell—does not seem to exude evil at a quick glance. And the truck's driver, a young man who was trying admirably to make child support payments for his young son and held down a steady job even in a crumbling county economy, did not eventually grow a pointy goatee or decide suddenly to dress smartly in red. I was sad for the quiet couple to move away, but Diamond seemed like a normal guy who would make a fairly decent neighbor. At first.

Subtlety is the tempter's forte. A Mephistopheles end-around. Slowly bore into the victim's unsuspecting brain a cloaked version of the very thing he is fleeing; in stages, artfully, and certainly not all at once. The incrementally raised volume from a truck tailpipe, from whisper to din over several months of weekend tinkering, will work nicely.

*

I was on my daily afternoon walk, steeling pastoral nerves for the monthly meeting of our church council that Monday evening, picking up trash along our road—mostly empty plastic soft drink bottles that kids were tossing out a moving school bus window, an impropriety difficult for one adult on the vehicle to monitor. I suspect there's a direct correlation be-tween bus driver longevity and Valium addiction.

Our neighbor, Betty, takes the lower half of the road. I take the upper half ending at the school. "Pasture," she says. "I just can't understand why anyone would litter. Littering is like soiling your own britches on purpose. This is God's great big beautiful world, our Mother Earth, and we're part and parcel of all of it, including this lovely road. We should love and respect this old momma of ours."

Gladys Welch tells me Betty can be a nerve-eater in their Ladies Circle meetings, but I've always liked her, especially when she pronounces the clergy title I tend to avoid like the open field in which we're instructed to recline in the twenty-third Psalm. She reminds me of a little bag lady I used to observe back in the city who collects discarded aluminum cans for her weekly livelihood. A warped pastoral colleague used to intentionally toss his Cheerwine cans in the ditch on Elmwood Avenue so she'd have a little extra change and feel good about her daily work. I sometimes wonder if the kids on the bus litter for similar reasons. Perhaps they enjoy watching Betty stoop and expose her wide posterior. But like the prophets of old, she delights in her righteous vision even as they yell at her.

That Monday, tending my end of our road, I found a dozen shredded pieces of notebook paper halfway up the hill to the school. What had once been a penciled message in a child's handwriting was now spread out hap-hazardly in the grass along the shoulder of the road, apparently discarded out the bus window. My curiosity got the best of me. After the walk, in my home office, I taped the pieces of the message together like a puzzle. Here's what it said, in large block letters that almost filled the page:

MOMMA DONT LUV MY DADDY ENNYMOR. I CAN TALE BYE THE WAY SHE LUKS AT HEM WHIN I GO SLEEP AT HIS HOSE ON WOODLND DRIVE AND SHE DROPS ME OFF THURE. SHE LUVS ANUTHER MAN WHO GETS MAD AT ME AND YELS AT ME AL THE TYME. I WISH I HAD SUMBODY TO TLK TO.

It didn't take Sherlock Holmes to identify the author of the note. And it made me feel even worse about what I was planning to do to my neigh-bor's truck.

We probably saw little Desmond Smoak at least as much as we heard Diamond. While his daddy tinkered on the truck in the garage, Desmond would wander over on weekends to chat with me and Catherine as we puttered around the yard, weeding her flowers or washing the car. He often eagerly offered to help. Maybe nine years old, Desmond was a cute little boy and loved to talk about almost anything, like a kid who hardly ever had anyone listen to him. He wore a Braves cap and overalls, just like his dad, almost every time I saw him. I wondered how he did in school, bouncing back and forth each weekend between parents.

"I was in church the other Sunday with my momma," he once said, "and the preacher told about Abraham and Isaac and their trip up that mountain? I bet y'all know that'n and if so, what do you make of that strange stow-ry?"

Catherine glared at me with eyes that could capture her prey with the exacting precision of that woodpecker I was telling you about. She didn't have to say it, but I knew she was remembering that time many years ago when our own son, Lukas, was hardly nine and walked into my study one afternoon as I was preparing for a sermon on the same story Desmond had just asked about—Genesis 22 if you want to look it up.

I'd been consulting a large coffee table book containing Rembrandt paintings of famous Bible narratives and the great artist was sparing no detail with this odd tale of a father and his only son. Isaac, just a boy, was dutifully prone on the Mount Moriah altar with his neck pulled back by his dad's huge paw of a hand in what seemed like an impossibly angled position. Rembrandt had powerfully captured the awful downward swoop of the knife. A ram was caught in a nearby bush. Lukas looked at the painting that day and then looked at me. "Daddy, why do you think God told Abraham to do such a thing to his son Isaac on that mountain?"

I let his question sink in and then for some strange reason said, "Because Isaac had been a bad little boy that day."

"Ohhh," said Lukas, wide-eyed and a bit panicked. I quickly hugged him, laughed, and said I was just kidding, of course. Only kidding! That's the day Catherine said, "You're all warped. Every last one of you. Some days I'm not sure why I married one."

So yes, those eyes were just daring me to answer Desmond's question the wrong way. I think I changed the subject. I could have said something about God testing us, but God knows I'd already failed in my own little neighborhood test.

*

I came across an interesting James Baldwin quote the other day in my personal reading and thought it might fit well in a sermon: "Nobody is more dangerous than he who imagines himself pure in heart, for his purity, by definition, is unassailable." I shared the quote with Catherine. She only looked at me and said, "Well, there you go." I wasn't sure what she meant by such a curt response.

It's hard to fully describe why or how the noise eventually made me into a madman on a mission, ready to break laws and further malign a neighbor's already shaky reputation. But there was something about the early morning intrusion into our sleep and my heretofore quiet lawn space that just seemed like Diamond was flaunting a flagrant "fuck you" at me every time he engaged the truck ignition. Difficult to ignore such an affront, even for a pastor.

Catherine says I'm imagining things, but on the front porch the other day, reading *The New Yorker*, I could have sworn he winked at me as he passed by, wiggling his left index finger out the open window of the cab, grinning like a Cheshire cat looking over the top of his sunglasses. I'd followed the advice about "turning the other cheek" my whole life, it seemed, and decided Jesus never lived next door to a loud truck or he wouldn't have offered such counsel.

My first planned offensive was meant to only be a loud warning across the bow. I'd wait until Diamond was in bed, string a long skein of speaker wire through our adjoining trees and across his lawn, and then blare "Sweet Home Alabama" through my new Amazon Echo Dot at absolutely full volume.

I'm kidding. Do you think I'm an idiot? Too much evidence.

The suspicion (and resulting blame) would need to be angular, clearly away from me, in other words. With Halloween around the corner, Catherine's students came to mind. Just the sort of prank a teenager would concoct.

*

I dressed all in black that moonless night (not a wardrobe stretch for a pastor), even removing the white neck tab on my clerical shirt. My only tools were a thin two-penny nail to let the air out of all four tires (through the valve stems, no lasting damage) and a bar of soap. I was a bit worried about masking the hissing sound emanating from a slowly flattened tire, but I tested just a squirt of release on one of my new front tires from Main Street Tire and Brake and figured out an almost inaudible method that would never be heard.

The soaped advice on the windshield troubled me a bit in terms of authenticity so I fished around at dinner that night, casually asking Catherine about the latest slang at her school and finally decided on "GET A LIFE, SMOAK." Short and sweet. I wasn't convinced Diamond could read much more than that anyway.

The neighborhood was blessedly quiet. I slipped out of bed with no notice from a slumbering Catherine and changed into my black get-up and night vision goggles I'd borrowed from a friend who'd served in the Green Berets, almost forgetting the gloves. It would be incredibly embarrassing for police to find a pastor's fingerprints adorning a crime scene.

The message traced with the bar of Ivory occurred first. It felt good to bear down and inscribe the thirteen letters several times for added emphasis. I noticed my teeth were clenched in a satisfying smirk. On to the four tires.

Kneeling on the driveway, just before pressing the nail into the first valve stem, I heard the back door to the garage creak open. I whispered a colorful expletive. There stood Desmond Smoak in his pajamas, looking at me curiously. "Hey, Pastor Greenway! Why are you out here right now? Can I help you with that?" Just like the little imp, always wanting to assist.

I recovered quickly. "Well, the question, young Desmond, is what *you* are up to at this hour. Aren't you supposed to be in bed for school tomorrow?"

"I thought I heard my raccoon trap go off and wanted to check it. There's been a coon gettin' in our garbage at night and Daddy said I could keep him if we caught one. Want to check and see if we caught old Rocky?"

And that was my "out" that dark night. Checking a raccoon trap with an innocent little boy. It wasn't that difficult getting Desmond back to bed without waking his father. We did pause and read the truck windshield together, washing off the graffiti. I didn't try to argue with Desmond when he said it was "probly those bad boys on my bus."

When I went out to get the paper the next morning, Diamond thanked me for helping his son wash the words off the windshield in the middle of the night.

"Don't mention it," I said. "That's what neighbors are for."

*

This whole sordid saga would have been a lot easier to forget had Catherine not come down with severe appendicitis two days later and the battery in our only car (a savvy ecological decision that niftily matches our last name) would not turn over. The Bradleys on the other side were at the beach so yes, *judge me*. I knocked on Diamond's door.

He was so eager to help it almost embarrassed me, glad for the porch's darkness. "Why sure, no problem, you take my truck on to the hospital. I need to stay here with little Desmond. He's asleep. But I don't even need my vehicle all weekend. Just keep it, pastor. Here are the keys. You can drive a stick, right? I sure hope Ms. Greenway will be all right. You git goin'."

Catherine was eventually just fine. Emergency surgery. A week out of school. I was the one who never completely recovered as we sped down Highway 28 towards the hospital with flashers and a noise that could indeed wake the dead in the cemetery we passed on the way.

That stupid song kept popping into my head. That song I really hate.

"I Drive Your Truck."

14.

Albert Higgins

WHEN ALBERT HIGGINS WAS a little boy he always dreamed of running away. He'd pack his small suitcase with a pair of clean underwear and a toothbrush and announce to the family at their long dinner table that it had been nice knowing them and all, but he was leaving for good this time. Usually, he walked about a quarter-mile to his Aunt Betty's house and spent the night with her. She left the front porch light on and the screen door unlatched when Albert's mother phoned ahead.

Betty would feed Albert blueberry pancakes the next morning, his favorite, and take him back home after the older children left the house and the school bus loudly departed the neighborhood. She loved her nephew and watched him wave goodbye from the driveway with his small right hand barely moving an inch either way. He always carried the suitcase like a proper little man. His brothers laughed at Albert when they found him home those afternoons. "Get too lonely for you out there on the open road?" they taunted.

The family all piled in the station wagon each summer and spent a week at the "Negro beach" on the South Carolina coast. Albert liked to walk down to the pier alone with his fishing rod and bait shrimp. It wasn't far. He sat on a backless bench at the middle of the pier near the breakers with his collar up and ball hat pulled down, leaned forward with his tennis shoes resting on a wooden slat, and pretended he was a runaway orphan, even when his brothers arrived a little later and laughed at him.

His line hung up on a pier pylon once. Albert was sure he'd hooked a big fish, calling loudly for someone to bring a net. A large crowd gathered around him and the little boy cranked his reel tautly, the pole bending like a rainbow. Albert was positive he had a state record flounder—notoriously weak-mouthed—on the line, requiring a careful landing. The hook finally gave way and flew upward with such force that it became tangled in an old woman's long silver hair. She'd been looking down at the water and screamed like she was dying, calling out for relatives who weren't there.

For days after they returned home, Albert's brothers tormented him with a three-word tease: *"Get the net!"* Several times that summer he reappeared at the dinner table with his little suitcase, vowing never to return.

On his eighteenth birthday, Albert was drafted. His suitcase had grown in size and so had he. This time he was sure he'd never return home again, but both legs were blown off in a wet jungle from a Viet Cong land mine. He collected disability payments and a wheelchair from the government, and for awhile lived alone in a small duplex apartment that had a porch light and a screen door that brought back good memories for a double amputee who told everyone who asked that he had no family.

Albert was kind to everyone he met, but prone to swallowing lies. He liked a good fish story and fell for the bait every time. Soon he lived on the street with his wheelchair and depended on our church for his food every night, served in the gym on long tables. Once a month Albert collected his check at the post office but that was quickly gone from friends who said they needed help. He never refused their requests, even when he knew they were taking advantage of him.

The church served blueberry pancakes for dinner one night. He sipped hot coffee with his street friends and a few church members until it was time to leave. Albert cried as he wheeled his chair from the light of the gymnasium and out into the damp darkness of the city, remembering his Aunt Betty.

*

Albert used to wear wrapped medical tape on his hands to prevent blisters, but eventually developed calluses immune to friction. I could've jabbed his palms with a straight pin and he wouldn't have flinched.

He zoomed down Sumter Street a lot faster than most people could run and easily navigated city traffic between the church and the capital building. "My turf, my home," he liked to say, roughly a square mile of noise and busy commerce until the darkening city quieted as downtown workers departed at day's end.

On weekday afternoons after work, motorists waiting in traffic rolled down their windows and called out to their smiling friend, a city celebrity of sorts. Every Christmas, people brought presents by the church for "that kind man in the wheelchair." Albert parked his chair on the sidewalk in front of the church sanctuary in the waning sunlight and greeted people when they honked with that same shy wave that never moved more than an inch in either direction.

Albert never asked the church for much. We replaced his wheelchair tires about every six months and had an arrangement with Bledsoe's Drugs two blocks away. They kept the tires in stock for Albert, who entertained customers during installation from his perch on three stacked pillows near the prescription window. Albert joked that he "got more mileage on my tires than any cripple in South Carolina and might be contacted any day to do a TV commercial for the tire company."

Elbert Bledsoe, the pharmacist, always gave Albert a squirt bottle of Ajax and two clean rags that he stowed in a cloth pouch on the back of the wheelchair. Elbert called the two of them "The Bert Brothers" and supplied Albert with everything he needed to clean tires and hubcaps for loose change in three nearby parking lots, including ours. You could often hear the little squirts from his spray bottle before actually seeing Albert, who usually exited his chair for the pavement, descending to eye level of the tire for more efficient cleaning. The legless man had amazing arm strength and could maneuver his body with the speed and agility of a gymnast.

He parked his wheelchair every Sunday morning right next to the baptismal font, after making the sign of the cross with fingers wet with sacramental water, and would eventually fall asleep sometime during my sermon. A few people complained about the volume of his snoring. I didn't care. Albert taught us more about heavenly trust than anything I could've mustered from the pulpit.

Once during the evening meal in the gym, Albert pulled into the serving line with a deep cut above his left eye, blood still seeping around the edges of the wound. He wouldn't talk about it. But his friends did. Alonzo, a tall and alarmingly thin man born in Savannah, shook with anger as he described the men "who fuckin' dared to beat up my friend in an alley just off of Bull Street last night. I don't know what you might think, Rev, but those punks will surely be judged by a pissed-off God and assigned to the hottest outback of Hades. What kind of lowlife would beat up and rob a man with no legs? Answer me that."

I had no answer for Alonzo's question but promised to look into the crime with one of our church members, Oliver Derrick, a deputy with the city police.

*

Our organist, Jim, introduced me to Albert soon after my arrival at Midlands Lutheran. Jim is a church musician but also a tireless advocate for social justice in the city. He regularly calmed older church members who thought the presence of homeless people on our property was "driving away fine young Christian families searching for Jesus but who are understandably afraid for the safety of their small children."

A wealthy woman named Dorothy Montgomery, married to a much older man who owned four different city blocks, stormed into the church office one weekday morning after a local choral concert we'd hosted for the community the previous Sunday afternoon. Albert and a couple of his friends had attended.

"The lectern was left out of place, the candlesticks on the altar were askew, and I can't find the candle lighter anywhere," Dorothy loudly complained. "I'm almost certain one of the homeless men took that holy and irreplaceable artifact and sold it down at Wally's Pawn Shop. Who knows where it might be now?"

Dorothy pronounced the words like many South Carolina women of her age and social position: *altah; lightah; ah-tifact.*

Jim had a hunch about the missing candle lighter. Only he and Dorothy possessed a key to a musty storage room in the basement of the old church. He hadn't looked in the room in years. Jim turned on the light and walked down a narrow passageway lined with old hymnals nobody had the heart to throw away. Leaning against the far wall in a mildewed corner was the "stolen" candle lighter.

To his enduring credit and my unceasing admiration, Jim reported the incident to the church council at our regular meeting later that month. When Dorothy heard about the accusation, she ceased monetary offerings for six months and vowed never to return to Midlands Lutheran. "I've no idea how the lighter found its way down there and find it laughable you misguided fools think I could stoop to such a thing."

I told Alonzo the candle lighter story one night at supper and he almost choked on a ham biscuit, laughing, quickly suggesting that Dorothy might wind up "down they-ah" with Albert's tormentors if the hellish story of Dives and Lazarus might apply also to a wealthy woman. Alonzo knew his Bible.

Soon after the mugging, Jim found Albert a very affordable apartment with the help of social services who said the disabled veteran qualified for numerous services he wasn't currently receiving; a "safety net" of sorts for people with Albert's challenges. The congregation helped furnish the small place, a safe home, away from and above the street. The entire church staff waited inside the sixth-floor apartment to surprise our friend with a little party on his move-in day. We'd stocked his new refrigerator with food. Albert never showed up. Instead, he mysteriously disappeared for two months.

*

"If you look closely in the shadows of each picture, with each arrest you'll notice the wheelchair. I can't say for sure it's Albert. Too dark outside. Maybe you can make out some of the details. He has no record, as far as I can tell, but Pastor, if this is Albert he's been associating with some pretty shady people. What's a bit odd to me is why he'd want to hang around long enough to make it into the photos. But there are always people milling about when one of the blue lights makes an arrest downtown at night. Nothing much else to do, I guess. I'll ask the officers of record to see if they might remember him."

I almost told Oliver there was no need to ask his fellow officers. In one of the shadowy photos, the back of the wheelchair revealed the cloth pouch carrying the tire cleaning materials. The nozzle of the Ajax spray bottle was clearly in view. It was Albert. But where was he now?

I walked with Oliver to the parking lot and his police car, thanked him for his time, and decided to walk around the block to the back of the church property and sit awhile in the morning sun to clear my head before the next appointment. A large southern live oak in the church courtyard provided ample shade for several homeless men on hot summer days, but this was February. All the benches in the courtyard were open. I zipped up my coat, sat down, and prayed awhile.

An incident that occurred in our adjacent church cemetery swam into my prayers. Last spring on a warm day, Dorothy Montgomery witnessed a homeless couple loudly making love among the tombstones and early daffodils in broad daylight. She reported it (in some detail) to the church council. During coital throes, the female shouted the name of a certain saint—Perpetua, I seem to recall Dorothy saying—accentuating The Heiress's moral revulsion. (That's what we called her around the church office.)

I sat in the council meeting that evening, listening to her rant against homeless people for the hundredth time, and concluded the sassy windbag was probably jealous of the graveyard ecstasy. It had surely been decades since Dorothy knew such rapture. Her husband, Ronald, was so old now that his waning energy only allowed him to count his money and offer Sunday morning death-stares to unruly children. I prayed for Dorothy also in the silence of the courtyard, a quiet place apart from the mid-morning bustle, even in the center of the city.

I didn't hear him. My eyes were closed and I felt the touch of rough fingers on folded hands. "If I didn't know better, Rev, from half a block away you looked a lot like 'Lonzo takin' a snooze on this old bench."

Albert smiled as if not a thing in the world was amiss, like he'd just had a stack of his Aunt Betty's blueberry pancakes.

*

Albert's behavior of engagement and retreat repeated itself with some frequency over the next months and into the summer. We'd help him wade through the red tape and all the frustrating forms that would surely have led to positive change in his life. But just before receiving a certain service that might help him, Albert would disappear and then resurface weeks later with that winning smile and no explanation. I wanted to throw a net over the slippery man and force him to comply with my pastoral understanding of a healthy life.

It's a story as old as Eden. It took me a long time to realize you can't "make" anyone do anything. If the desire for change isn't there, you may as well throw in the towel on anything from marriage to weight management, and even the presence of confessed desire for a new direction doesn't always spell success. Change can be hellish, even if it's for the good.

One of Albert's brothers, Jacob, called the church office one afternoon. I'm still not sure how he knew to call us. I arranged a meeting between the two of them and they hit it off after over two decades of sibling estrangement. With the blessing of Jacob's wife, Millie, Albert even moved to Augusta and lived for awhile in an apartment attached to their house, redesigned for easier accessibility. Jacob called me during this period and reported how his three young daughters loved and doted upon Albert, amazed at how fast their legless uncle could climb the large maple tree in the front yard. He would lie on his back in the grass and help the girls with their gymnastic routines with his strong arms. I really thought Albert had found a permanent home.

And then Oliver Derrick pulled into the church parking lot one unusually cold January morning as I was getting out of my car. "I didn't want to call you about this, Pastor. Thought I should tell you in person. Don't know how to tell you this except to just say it. A patrolman buddy of mine found Albert's body about 3:00 this morning on top of the parking deck three blocks from here. Somebody phoned in an anonymous tip. The roof of the parking deck, you know, is usually closed in the winter." Oliver paused and gave me some time to digest the information. I placed my briefcase down on the pavement and leaned against his squad car. He's a good friend, an excellent policeman.

"Not sure how long he'd been up there," Oliver continued. "Looked like he'd been beaten up pretty bad. His chair was nowhere to be seen. Somebody wrapped the body in a blanket and pushed it against a wall. They at least knew he'd be found eventually. Your friend's down at the morgue right now if you want to see him. I've cleared permission. They'll let you in."

I walked into the church office and called Jacob. Albert had vacated the apartment in Augusta in early December. No note of explanation.

*

We decided to have a memorial service for Albert. Dozens of Albert's homeless friends attended and not a few city commuters who'd known the kind man who waved at them on the corner in front of the church. Oliver was there, out of uniform, with a few other patrolmen who'd come to care about Albert.

It was amazing how word spread about the late afternoon service after we posted simple flyers on several telephone poles and kiosks within a couple blocks of the church. Even Dorothy Montgomery showed up and sat in the back, mostly to assess damage to the building afterwards. Albert's nieces sat with their parents on the front row. No one else from Albert's family chose to attend, even though Jacob called each of them to report the news.

We sang an opening hymn, "There's A Wideness in God's Mercy," and I decided to use one of my favorite stories from the Gospel of John, chapter twenty-one, an Easter story even though it was still in the middle of winter. I stood near the baptismal font to deliver the sermon, where Albert often parked his wheelchair.

"And you know those disciples were not supposed to be out there in the first place," I said. "Jesus had given clear instructions to leave their nets, follow him, and fish for people. But there they were, out in the middle of the night, back at their old jobs, their old way of life."

Several of Albert's friends nodded vigorously and Alonzo offered a loud "Uh-huh, sounds about right!"

Even from where she was sitting, I could see Dorothy Montgomery rolling her eyes. I fleetingly had the urge to stride down the aisle of the church and slap that woman.

"It's often difficult to change," I continued, "and take a new direction even when you know it's the right thing to do. Albert spent much of his money and some of his time on the wrong things with the wrong people. It's an old story. And it's more than just assigning blame, someone's fault who wasn't strong enough to change."

An older woman with no teeth shouted, "You got that right, Reverend! We talkin' 'bout that old devil! Lucifer hisself out there waitin' on us!"

Dorothy got up to leave. I waited until the old front door of the church closed to quiet the brief noise from the city traffic and said, "There goes somebody out the door to meet him now." Alonzo put his hand over his mouth and placed his head between his knees, his body shaking with laughter. The moment broke any remaining ice.

For the next thirty minutes, people stood up from where they were sitting to tell a story about Albert—a kindness, a sacrifice, a funny incident. Their stories were the real sermon that day. I hardly had to mention that Jesus was the sort of guy who threw a breakfast on the beach for people caught doing the wrong thing.

We shared the bread and wine around the font and sang "Amazing Grace" by heart. On the way down to the gym for supper, most of us dipped fingers in the water and made the sign of the cross. One man stood quietly for a moment at the edge of the font, confused, then bent down and washed his whole head, beard dripping and face radiant as he came up from the water.

We all walked down the old wooden stairs into the light of the gymnasium. Waiting for us were blueberry pancakes.

*

I think about Albert a lot these days during my walks around the neighborhood. He loved this city, loved living free on the streets; his home by choice after a point.

Jacob came by the church one morning while in the city on business downtown. We talked awhile in my office and he took me to lunch around the corner at a deli called The No-Name.

"It's odd that we're eating here," he says. "You helped me retrieve Albert's name from my own past. I thought it was lost."

Jacob tells me the incident of the net at the beach, getting hooked on the pier pylon, and other stories about their family. He laughs, but wonders if he and his brothers were too hard on Albert when he was a little boy. I shake my head and tell him about a couple times I tormented my own little brother, even backing the boy against the wall of our carport, spreading his arms and legs, and tossing darts between the spaces like those guys in the circus. One stuck in his lower calf.

Jacob snorts and says, "At least the two of us didn't behave like Joseph's crazy brothers in the book of Genesis. Those clowns sold their little brother into slavery!"

I laugh and say, "Albert surely loved you, Jacob."

We shake hands outside the deli and say goodbye. I have a little time and drive west on the interstate and take the exit Jacob described at lunch. No gas stations or restaurants in either direction. I encounter only two other cars in the ten miles and several turns into the country through the sand hills. It strikes me again how much natural beauty is so close to the city.

The house is still there, just as Jacob said. I park and decide to walk the quarter-mile to Betty Higgins's place, now abandoned and needing a new roof. Several silent birds perch on a wire above the road. A large oak tree dwarfs the bare front yard. I try to imagine a little boy climbing the steps with his small suitcase.

Albert stops at the door, turns, and smiles.

His hand is open and shyly waving, moving slowly, only a single inch in either direction.

15.

Bus Number Six

PASTOR NEWRY DERRICK HAD requested Number Seven for his new school bus route up the mountain to the community of Snake Creek, in the western part of the county, because it was the perfect number in the Bible. But seven was taken, so he settled for six, seeing how he needed the money due to the hefty annual budget cut at New Mount Carmel Lutheran Church.

"Holy shit," Newry whispered, consecrating his expletive and blowing warm air from the bellows of bearded jowls onto fingers that felt frozen. He cranked Number Six (the oldest bus in an aging district fleet) on the first day back to school after the long Christmas break. At 6:15 AM it was still dark in January, a beautiful starry sky, as he pulled onto Highway 28 leading up the mountain. The planet Venus twinkled in the east as the first hint of a new day began to outline ancient oak trees on the ridge above Deadman's Curve.

"My granddaddy Roy would have a cow if he knew I was driving a bus marked with the 'devil's digit,' but a man's gotta feed his family," Newry told his wife, Claire, earlier that morning over coffee. A recent graduate of the county tech school with an emphasis in hairstyling, she worked part-time at Ovaline's Cuts and Curls in Buena Vista. But the two salaries combined weren't covering the bills in a household with three young boys who seemed to need new shoes every other month.

The young pastor loved his church and loved his family. And he loved the land over which the aging bus (with tears in almost every vinyl seat) now traveled. He knew that his salary reduction at New Mount Carmel had more to do with the local economy and a factory closure than with his pastoral performance, but it still hurt.

Newry sometimes wondered if the education difference between himself and his parishioners created a wedge of resentment. He loved words and books and knew it was probably time to dial back the vocabulary he used in Sunday sermons. Many of his parishioners had not graduated from high school and could not care less what the word *eschatology* meant.

Just before his first stop, a shooting star raced across the width of the bus windshield. Newry pondered the possible relationship between the words *cosmology* and *cosmetology*. He treasured the music of language and how words made sounds as lovely as water flowing over smooth creek stones. A small child waving a flashlight woke the minister from his word-stem reverie.

The double doors swung open. A boy who looked to be in the second grade climbed up the two tall steps into the warmth of the bus. He wore a small backpack, a heavy coat several sizes too large, and an orange toboggan hat. "Well, good morning, young man. My first passenger! I'm Pastor Newry, your new bus driver. I'm sure you heard about Mr. Samuelson."

Little Jimmy Campbell had not heard about Robert Samuelson, the former bus driver of Number Six, who'd moved to Florida in mid-December to live closer to his adult children. It seemed strange to Newry that a bus driver hadn't shared this with the students, but maybe Jimmy had been absent from school on the last day before the break.

"No, he told us Santa had been watchin' and hoped we'd been more nice than naughty since last Christmas, but he didn't say nothin' about movin' away to no Floridee." Jimmy was a talkative child, especially for a little boy who'd just met a stranger.

"My daddy said Mr. Sam's a queer but he says that about a lot of people. My daddy gits mad easy. One time he hit my momma."

Number Six's route was the most remote and mountainous in the county. With four miles to the next stop, Jimmy talked almost without taking a breath, until Mary Jane Moore stepped on the bus.

"I'm a third-grader," she told Newry after he asked. Jimmy reminded Newry of his own little boys who clammed up even around the girls they knew well from church.

When he dropped Jimmy off at his driveway later that Monday after school, the bus was even louder than he'd anticipated from the voices of twenty-six children who'd "just been released from jail," according to one fifth-grader.

Newry watched the little boy as he ran up the steep gravel driveway towards an old cabin that needed a new roof. Smoke rose from a chimney. The orange toboggan hat bobbed up the ridge like a small rabbit until Newry lost sight of it amidst the rhododendron.

*

The next morning, a Tuesday, Newry arrived twenty minutes early to top off Number Six, a notorious guzzler. Since the day after Christmas, the feast of Stephen, when he sketched out elevation changes along his route with the assistance of a topography map, Newry realized he should never run out of diesel fuel in the mountains.

He'd always wondered why a Christian martyr's death date was celebrated so close to the Lord's nativity, vowing in almost the same breath "not to sacrifice my life to the county school system by getting stuck near nightfall on Blind Jack Ridge Road."

According to Jeremy Lane, a parishioner who headed the county narcotics office, the unpaved forest service cut-through was rather infamous for drug deals gone awry. "More than one blind jackass has lost his life for heroin stupidity on Blind Jack," Jeremy said after church one Sunday. Even so, the road could easily serve as a convenient shortcut over to Highway 28 after dropping off Newry's last student. "I know it saves you time," Jeremy said. "But keep your eyes open on that road, especially after dark."

The bus driver corps had also been summoned that Tuesday morning to a short meeting in the school cafeteria. Newry and a dozen older men gathered around Wanda Thompson, the only female driver at Cora B. Yates Elementary. She'd brought along a copy of the 1929 *Foothills Garden Pine Burr*, the local high school yearbook featuring her grandfather's senior class, and was describing an officially sanctioned group called "The Dumpye Club," an actual campus organization for overweight people long before the days of political correctness. Their motto, printed in the yearbook under a group photo: *"Eatybus, drynkybus sed non bustybus."* The men howled at the yearbook pictures of large people eating their favorite foods, which seemed strange to Newry since he guessed most of them probably had a hard time climbing the two steps to their bus driver seats.

The purpose of the meeting was to warn drivers that the heaters on many of the aging buses would sometimes malfunction. "There's not a lot to be done," said Wanda, who'd regained her composure as lead driver after the yearbook laughter had subsided, "except ride out the morning and limp on back to maintenance after you discharge your bus students for class. Even on a warm afternoon during the winter months I'd keep all the windows up, tight as a drum, to bank a bit of warm air just in case. Four or five degrees of warmth can feel pretty good to these young uns. Some of 'em go from a cold house to a cold driveway, waiting on us."

Wanda sent the drivers off with a short reading from the *South Carolina State Manual for Accredited Drivers*. "School bus drivers," she loudly quoted, "carry small but important packages of live cargo, precious children, which can 'shift' easily." Wanda looked up from the manual. "Amen to that, right, gentlemen?"

The fourteen drivers refilled coffee cups, bundled up with scarves and ball hats, and headed out to the roaring parking lot—the buses warming up, preparing for departure. As if on cue, Newry climbed into Number Six and discovered a bus cabin that wasn't much warmer than his front yard. He sanctified the interior with another choice expletive. "The pastor's extensive vocabulary lacks an editor," Claire once told him.

Newry double-checked the contents of the vehicle's First Aid Kit, and made a note of the respective expiration dates on the Body Fluid Cleanup Kit and small fire extinguisher. He wondered if one of the women's circles at his church might donate a box of winter gloves for his bus. It would be an especially frigid morning without heat in Foothills Garden, South Carolina.

*

Newry was glad he had a warm coffee cup to shift back and forth between cold hands. The juggling act was made a bit easier with fewer gear changes due to a slow farm truck he followed on the way up the mountain to Jimmy's driveway. He noticed a crass bumper sticker in the headlights and was glad he didn't have to explain it to his ever-curious passengers.

"LICK HER UP," the sticker blared in all caps, a rather warped play on words from the boisterous campaign-rally chants of the country's new president, who carried Foothills Garden and vicinity with an astounding 75 percent of the vote. Newry was again especially confounded how Christians (Lutherans!) seem to have been a key factor in electing the man.

Jimmy's dad, Clarence, was standing with his young son at the end of the Campbell driveway. The same orange toboggan hat was poking out of a large bed quilt wrapped around the boy and his father. Clarence wore a hat featuring a logo with the large head of a smiling pig. The doors opened and even though the bus's lack of warmth was obvious as Jimmy, shivering, found his seat, his dad never offered to relinquish the quilt.

"Hey there, Rev! I hear you're the new bus driver for the Snake Creek co-munity. Welcome, sir! What'd they do over at your church, cut the pastor's salary? Ha-ha! Lookee here, you're not gonna believe this, but I hear tell there's a Sasquatch heathen in these hills. You best watch the shadows in the early a.m. when you round the curves in this old jay-lopy."

Since arriving at New Mount Carmel, Newry had heard sensational tales about the eight-foot beast roaming the mountains above Foothills Garden. He hoped Clarence hadn't noticed his eye roll in the light of the bus cabin. New for Newry was any suspect religious affiliation for the beast.

Newry tried to clarify. "Did you say a *heathen* Sasquatch?"

"No, I said he was heathen!"

"That's what I'm asking. How could it matter whether the Sasquatch is heathen or not? What could religion possibly have to do with this?"

"Look, Rev. You're not hearin' me right. HEATHEN, I'm tellin' you. Let me spell it out. H-I-D-D-N. He's a wily and slippery man-beast!"

"*Hidden*. Okay. A rather elusive Sasquatch. Got it. I'll be on the lookout."

"You take care of my boy now, you hear? There's a lot in these mountains that's out to get people like us. Am I right, Rev?"

Newry wasn't about to disagree. He closed the doors, took off his coat and wrapped it around the little boy, and headed down the curving road as the sun broke through the trees. Jimmy talked a mile a minute, but his teeth didn't stop chattering until they reached Mary Jane Moore's driveway.

*

One of the young mothers at New Mount Carmel asked Newry the following Sunday if he ever raced any of the other bus drivers back to the school on weekday mornings. "Hey, we raced all the time on my old route when I was a sixteen-year-old driver in high school," Lori Rogers said at the church door. "It's a wonder the cops didn't stop me for speeding or running the occasional stop sign. The crazy kids on my bus egged me on with a stopwatch. I was stupid. It was a hard job sometimes. Had to throw an older kid off the bus once; this big guy who was about twice my size. But I loved it for the most part—a little extra money. Some of the parents used to wait at my stops and give me cookies and cornbread every once in awhile."

Newry couldn't imagine Jimmy Campbell's dad giving him much of anything but a hard time. Clarence motioned him to get out of the bus the next morning as Jimmy sat in the second row of Number Six with its newly repaired heater. Technically, by the manual, Newry was never supposed to exit the bus during his route, especially with a child inside, but he was running early and Clarence looked a little irked.

"Lookee here, padre. I seen you wrap up little Jimmy with your fancy winter coat last week. You tryin' to make his daddy look bad or somethin'? That kid's about as spoiled as they come. A little cold won't hurt him."

Clarence's four missing teeth probably made him appear more menacing than he'd intended. Newry decided to get back on the bus slowly. He couldn't decide whether to tell the school principal, Velma Powers, about the whiskey he'd smelled on Mr. Campbell's breath at 6:47 AM.

*

A little later that January Newry had a minor unavoidable accident, largely caused by afternoon snow flurries that at one point became almost blinding in their intensity. He pulled off the road at a scenic overlook above Foothills Garden that usually offered a nice view of the town.

The kids on the bus, every seat taken, were excited by the snow, a rarity in South Carolina. Town residents often said that frozen precipitation could be predicted if the weather vane atop New Mount Carmel Church was pointing towards the post office. But this snow came completely out of the blue. Newry had to quiet his elementary school kids who all wanted to exit the bus for a snowball fight.

The snow subsided after ten minutes, with parting clouds, and the bus resumed its steep climb up the mountain toward Snake Creek. Newry felt the bus slide a bit as he descended a steep hairpin turn near Grove Spring, these days a cluster of mostly abandoned buildings. Newry knew not to hit the brakes even though he'd been told Number Six had an anti-lock feature.

He turned the front wheels in the direction of the vehicle's slow slide. The bus came to rest astride a shallow ditch. Newry gently engaged the accelerator, only once, and felt the rear of the bus settle further into the mud. An older Grove Spring resident (the last remaining citizen of the little community, Newry later learned) appeared on a front porch across the road and called out to see if he could phone for help. The kids on Bus Number Six would all be a little late for supper that evening.

Clarence Campbell was waiting for the bus at the end of the driveway when it pulled up in the last thirty minutes of afternoon light. "I was beginnin' to wonder if I should trust my boy to some no-count preacher who don't even know how to drive." Clarence was grinning as he said the words but it had been a long day and Newry's patience was already razor-thin from extended containment with twenty-six children.

"Yeah, and I'm starting to wonder if I should let Jimmy's teachers know that his father appears regularly at the bus stop smelling like a brewery." Newry regretted the words as soon as they left his mouth. Jimmy heard them, standing beside his dad. Other children on the bus laughed. The little boy looked stricken and took a step back from his father, almost slipping in a patch of snow now turning to ice in the falling darkness.

Newry couldn't get Clarence's eyes out of his mind as he delivered the remaining twenty-five children to their destinations. The man had stared at Newry with narrowing slits that conveyed a pure and wordless hatred.

Some parents whose children were usually last off the bus drove to closer stops, shortening the route. Almost every parent thanked Newry for his time and for keeping their children safe. One mother handed him a cup of hot coffee and a box of donuts from Krispy-Kreme.

The young pastor knew the shortcut over to Highway 28 might be a bit muddy but he was ready to get home to Claire and the boys. When the sign marking Blind Jack Ridge appeared in his headlights, Newry slowly turned the bus hard to the left, leaving the pavement and the last streetlight he'd see for the next seven miles.

*

The principal at Cora B. Yates, Velma Powers, was close to retirement that winter. A small faculty group had already started planning a staff party on an evening in June that would coincide with her final commencement ceremony. She'd spent her entire career at the school and taught fourth grade across the hallway from young Clarence Campbell when he was ten.

Velma served on the call committee that brought Newry to New Mount Carmel. He'd liked her from the beginning. She didn't patronize a recent seminary graduate with dumb questions about his age and apologized privately the following December for the deep cuts in the church spending plan. She was always a straight shooter.

"Look, I know you didn't sign up for this when you arrived, but would you be interested in driving one of my buses? If you don't like it, you can always quit. And who knows? Maybe the experience will give you a more accurate look at our county to help shape your ministry among us. God knows some of these Lutherans need their eyes opened to the challenges right here in the church neighborhood."

Soon after taking the new job, he parked the bus for the day, swept out the trash in Number Six, and knocked on the principal's door. Newry knew he could confide in Velma.

"Pastor Derrick," she smiled, ever the teacher. "Get in here and tell me what you've learned about our county children by driving that bus."

Newry briefly described his concern for Jimmy Campbell.

"Isn't that the cutest child you'll ever meet? It's hard for me to enforce the no-hats rule here at school when I see that little imp wearing his orange toboggan at the water fountain. I'm not surprised you noticed that about his dad. Clarence was a rounder even in the fourth grade. Came from a broken home with an alcoholic father. Tragic."

"Here's a funny story about Clarence, though. When he was a senior in high school one of my teacher friends said he tried to grow a beard, so many of his classmates called him 'Furball.' But one younger kid mistakenly called him *Fubar* one day. You know, the military acronym? And to my knowledge that's what most people in Snake Creek still call him today. The man can't do anything right. Social services is watching Jimmy's home life. Clarence has been warned. But don't cross him. That's my advice. He's got a mean streak."

Newry recalled Velma's advice as he drove along the spine of Blind Jack Ridge, regretting his words earlier that afternoon. The clouds had cleared and a new moon rose over the tree line. Newry realized that he could probably make a higher salary in downtown Columbia as an associate pastor at some large church, but Foothills Garden was surely a beautiful part of the state. And Velma had been right about the bus route exposing him to county needs he'd probably never see from the vantage point of the church office. Maybe God needed him right where he was for a reason.

Halfway down the cut-through road, just past a historic marker describing the existence of a nearby Cherokee village in the early part of the eighteenth century, Newry heard two loud pops and had to pull off onto a grassy berm. He found a flashlight in the emergency kit behind the driver's seat. "Great," he said out loud. "Just what I needed."

Jackrocks ("caltrops," in the dictionary) are usually associated with union activity, used by disgruntled workers to get the attention of management higher-ups. One of Newry's seminary classmates once described their mayhem in the coalfields of West Virginia during a massive mining layoff. A jackrock works especially well in a driveway, positioned just behind one or both rear wheels.

The pastor heard the slow hiss from two of the bus tires and could not believe someone had tossed a handful of the pointy devils on a forest service road, or that they could possibly do their mischief on such soft ground. Nor could he imagine who would hatch such hatred until he remembered a hiking trail connecting Jimmy's house to this point on Blind Jack Ridge. A person could walk here from the Campbell house much faster than he could drive.

Newry was looking at a three-mile hike out to Highway 28; an hour if he walked fast. Claire would be worried. Newry stopped appreciating the beauty of the new moon and yelled a choice word, this time unconsecrated, towards the night sky. Maybe there was something indeed sinister about the number of his bus.

The pastor headed down the dark road with the flashlight for twenty yards before going back to the bus to retrieve the remaining donuts from the Krispy Kreme box. Not the best of suppers, but he was hungry.

*

The next morning, Clarence was all smiles at the end of the driveway as he waited with Jimmy. "Sure hope you got home okay yesterdee evenin', padre. We're not used to snow here in South Carolina. Me and Jimmy included you in our bedtime prayers. Right, son?"

Jimmy looked at Newry as he boarded the bus, but didn't answer.

"You know, I've been thinkin' about somethin', Rev. Say a man was dyin'. No chance of makin' it even with the best medicine man in these New-nited States. If thar's two buttons in front of you at that point, and one sez DIE and you could push that button right then and thar, would you mash it?" Clarence let the question hang in the air for a moment.

"I tell you what I'd do. I'd mash that sumbitch and go right on to my maker."

The bus started to slowly move down the road and Newry closed the doors. "But what would *you* do, Reverend?! That's what I want to know! WHAT WOULD YOU DO?!!" Clarence's voice echoed across the hollow even over the bus's engine roar.

Newry looked into the rearview mirror and noticed Jimmy was crying. The little boy pulled the orange toboggan over his eyes and was quiet all the way to Mary Jane Moore's driveway.

*

Claire reached over in bed that night to touch Newry, who was reading about how to eradicate fire ants from their backyard. The ants had taken the newcomers by surprise during their first year in Foothills Garden. Newry was determined that wouldn't happen again. Fire ant stings could be dangerous, especially with young children. Even in the middle of winter, the young pastor was preparing his small fortress for all-out war on the wiggly invaders.

"There's this kid on my bus, a fifth-grader named Lucius, who told me to forget about the store-bought stuff. 'Pastor Newry,' he said, 'I like to pour gas on 'em.'"

Newry stopped a moment, smiled, and said to Claire, "The word rhymed with *vase* when Lucius described this gasoline process."

"'And then I strike a match and watch 'em burn,' the little fellow told me. 'Far works just as good on them ants. And they turn to ash. It won't hurt the earth. Ash is good for the soil. Just put a little gas on the mound and light her up. It's a lot more fun than them gran-yules. And a good bit cheaper, my daddy tells me.'"

Newry smiled. "Lucius pronounced 'ash' with a long *a*. I love those kids."

Claire looked at her husband. She knew he'd been worried about church. And now various children on his bus. "I'd like to light a 'far' in my man right now," Claire said as she tickled one of Newry's thighs.

After Newry got up to pee later that night, he looked out the window into the darkened backyard and decided to put on his robe and Crocs and tiptoe onto the back deck. A small snowman, constructed by the boys without his help, leaned crookedly to the left in the moonlight. A pointy carrot dangled precariously from the snowman's face and a big floppy hat almost rested on slushy shoulders.

Newry looked at the stars for several minutes and picked out the Big Dipper and the Pleiades cluster, which reminded him of their Subaru station wagon and how much he loved traveling with his little family. He watched the stars for some time and offered, with open eyes, a grateful prayer to God for bringing them to a new town. Newry gazed up at the night sky until his attention was suddenly drawn back to the snowman, now in a heap from its silent collapse.

*

Early the next week, Newry made another appointment with Velma Powers for Tuesday afternoon after school.

No one had been at the end of the Campbell driveway when he dropped off Jimmy, that day or the previous. The little boy almost looked relieved. Due to the warmth of the afternoon sun, he carried his orange toboggan in one hand and with the other waved back at Newry after safely crossing the road. Velma was right. An exceptionally cute kid. Newry didn't like to think about what his small friend faced each day after arriving home.

After releasing his last student, Newry had a bit of time to think about what he'd say to Velma. The appointment wasn't until 4:30, so he decided to take the long way back to the school. He loved the relative quiet of the bus late in the afternoon. The ride back to Yates Elementary gave him plenty of time to pray for each of his students by name.

The image of the fire ants also raced through his head. "Leave those suckers alone," he thought to himself, "and they'll just multiply." Newry was a pastor, but even a pastor is not immune to dark plans of imaginary retaliation. He smiled at the various ways he might get back at Clarence Campbell who'd all but admitted, with his sarcastic smile, to flattening two bus tires.

Clarence reminded Newry of Ernest T. Bass, that crazy unhinged character who occasionally showed up out of the mountains in Mayberry on early evening television. There was surely something redeemable about Clarence but Newry had yet to figure out what that might be.

Newry settled into a chair in Velma's office. Her secretary said she was tied up in another meeting and would arrive shortly. Instead of the usual framed accolades and various matted diplomas, Velma's walls were filled with the faces of children alongside an accompanying picture of the child grown into an adult. Newry didn't hear Velma enter the office. She spoke from behind him.

"Sometimes," she said, "you just can't tell how a child is going to turn out. I've taught kids who had every possible advantage and wound up in jail. I visited a woman last week at the state penitentiary in Columbia while attending a meeting in the city. We still write each other. She won't be getting out anytime soon. You'd never have predicted such a life. And that picture you're looking at now? That little boy grew up in some of the worst home conditions you could possibly imagine. And now he's a high school physics teacher in Florida. I've stopped trying to guess how kids will turn out. It's certainly other adults in their lives. And God, of course, Newry. We both believe in grace and providence, right? But maybe, sometimes, it's just bad luck. Or good luck. I'm not sure anymore."

When Newry turned around to face Velma, he was crying.

"I came in here this afternoon to talk with you about Clarence Campbell. I'm pretty sure it was Clarence who was behind the foolishness with the bus on the ridge road the other night. And Jimmy looks so unhappy these days. I wanted to ask your opinion about contacting law enforcement; maybe Jeremy Lane could help. But looking at your wall here changed my mind about what to do next."

Newry took out a handkerchief to blow his nose. "I always used to wonder why the school system didn't give teachers time to visit in the homes of their students. Looks like you've done a good bit of that. Well, what's stopping *me*? Clarence doesn't like me. I can tell that. But what's wrong with knocking on their door in Snake Creek and trying to find out a bit more about this family? Maybe trying to help them?"

Velma smiled as she came from behind the desk to hug her pastor. "That's a great idea, Newry. I can't think of another driver in our bus fleet who's done that, but you have my full support. And it may help. But before you go, I think there's something you need to know."

*

Bus Number Six pulls onto the grassy shoulder of Blind Jack Ridge near the Cherokee monument. The driver sits alone in silence. He prays for several minutes, head bowed against the large wheel that guides his children safely to their homes. The bus reminds the driver of a temporary home of sorts, where children look out windows and ponder the successes and hurt feelings of the day, perhaps catching their reflection in the window, a glimpse of who they are and who they might become. The children on the bus attempt to impress or humiliate one another in the subtle art of superiority modeled from older kids, constantly one-upping each other in playful and hurtful ways. They trust the driver up front, like a surrogate parent, to navigate safe passage through the many bends in a winding road. His prayers include gratitude and grace for each child, slowly named down thirteen rows of the large metal rolling rectangle, concluding with a certain boy who wears an orange hat and waves to the driver each afternoon; a wave with a small open hand, resembling a reach for help.

*

Newry pulls on his boots and shoulders his backpack, a warm day in early February. He can't recall what the groundhog observed two days ago but today certainly indicates an early spring and that's just fine with the novice bus driver.

The trail leading away from the forest service road hasn't been walked in awhile. He brushes back fallen limbs with his walking stick and stops once to take a long drink of water. The pack is heavier than it was on the last scouting overnight he led with several other fathers and their sons. Claire helped him load it. She knew he'd be later than usual getting home.

The clearing behind the Campbell cabin is open and bare in spots, nothing that resembles a yard, with evidence of recent stumps suggesting the need for heat inside. The trail emerges from the woods near a dog pen with an overturned water bowl and a gaping hole in the chicken wire. Newry guesses that Jimmy had a puppy at one time, but gratefully sees no sign of a dog who might announce his arrival.

During the minute he takes to walk through the clearing to the cabin, Newry again imagines Clarence's angry eyes that day at the bus stop. Distracted, he almost steps on an old, inactive mound of fire ants and kicks it instead with the toe of his boot.

Two shaky steps up the porch and a knock. Newry slides out of his pack and leans it against a stack of firewood. No one answers at first and he wonders about the last time anyone may have knocked. Jimmy's face appears in the window and his eyes widen with a smile that helps bring Newry's pulse down to near normal. The little boy opens the door and, without a word, grabs Newry with a tight hug around his bus driver's right leg.

"Where's your hat?" Newry asks. "It's a warm day, I know, but I'm not used to seeing you without it. Aren't you going to invite me in?"

Through the door and into the next room, Newry sees the legs of a man whose rocking has suddenly stopped. Beside his feet rests a bottle. Beyond the chair is a hospital bed with a woman under a single sheet, her head on two pillows. Her eyes open partially when she hears the boy greet what sounds like a guest.

The man in the chair resumes his rocking and, with his right foot, slowly slides the corked bottle behind a large pot containing a dead plant.

"Well you're here, ain't ya? Why don't you come on in?"

Clarence doesn't move from his chair when Newry extends his hand. An unwashed odor rises from the rocker. "Well, lo and Lordy behold. It's the bus driver. What brings you here among us this fine day, padre? You been missin' me at the bus stop?"

"Just thought I'd drop by. Velma Powers told me about your wife. I'm very sorry to hear about her illness."

"Yeah, well, we're all sorry. She's been a good old girl." Clarence raised his voice. "Hadn't ya', Sally?"

Sally Campbell raises one hand a couple inches off the bedsheet, drops it, and manages a smile.

"The hor-spice people come once a week but there ain't anything to be done really. It's the cancer." Clarence pronounces the word with the long *a* that Newry has come to love.

"It's little Jimmy we worry about now. I know you like my boy. And I want to 'pologize for bein' such a horse's ass. I just seem to mess up all the time. I'm sure you've heard tell about my nickname in these parts. But Jesus says you have to fer-give me, right? Ain't there sumthin' about that in your book, Rev?"

"Yes, Clarence, there is." Newry smiled. "And you can rest assured that I've screwed up my share of times."

"Well, there ain't been much restin' around this cabin for awhile since Sally got sick. But I think I like you, padre. Never heard no clergyman say the word *screw* before."

Newry laughed. "My wife will tell you I've let loose with a lot worse than that. Listen, I hope you won't take this the wrong way, but I brought you a few things and hope you can use them. It's from my whole family. I have three boys and know they sure can eat. Clarence, do you have a church that ever looks in on you all up here in Snake Creek?"

"A church? Good Gawd a-mighty! What church would want the Campbells?"

"Look, I know we're down in Foothills Garden and don't expect you to make it on Sundays, especially with what you're going through here, but we want you. And God wants you. I'm not one of those 'get-your-life-together-or-you're-going-to-hell' sort of preachers. Hope that doesn't disappoint you. Maybe we could help you through some of this."

Sally, who'd been listening, smiled at her husband and motioned Jimmy to the bedside.

"Well, yeah, Reverend. That might be nice. You drop in here whenever you like."

Clarence rose from the rocking chair and joined his family at the bed. Darkness was falling outside. The last rays of sun on a February afternoon brought another surprise to Newry.

"Lookee here, I know you need to be gettin' back down the mountain. You hiked up through them woods, right?" Clarence looked away and down at the floor.

"I'm wondrin' somethin'. If you're gonna be our preacher from now on, would you say a little prayer for our family before you leave us?"

Newry made his way to Sally's side of the bed. He looked at Jimmy, who could not hide a grin, and then nodded at the little boy's parents.

"I'd be honored to pray with you. In our church, we hold each other's hands when we pray. Is that all right with you?"

*

With no moonlight to help guide his way, Newry was glad he had a flashlight as he walked on the trail back to the bus. His pack felt lighter and so did his heart. He hummed an old hymn as he picked his way along the path, "The Day You Gave Us, Lord, Has Ended."

Newry knew there would be children to feed and bathe and tuck in when he arrived home. The day was far from over for him and Claire, but he loved this hymn—partly because evening hymns like this one didn't make the Sunday morning cut at New Mount Carmel—and offered a favorite verse to the surrounding woods as the very last hints of pink graced a clear and starry sky.

The sun, here having set, is waking
Your children under western skies,

And hour by hour, as day is breaking,
Fresh hymns of thankful praise arise.

A barred owl hooted as he finished singing and Newry laughed out loud, wondering if that meant he was off key or maybe in tune. For the first time in his ministry since arriving in Foothills Garden, he thought maybe it was the latter.

He reached the road and before boarding the old vehicle, looked skyward and sang the entire hymn, softly, one final time, as a prayer. He closed his eyes after the hymn and listened to the sounds of the forest until the chill of the evening caused him to climb into the driver's seat.

The bus made its way down the gravel road, eventually connecting with Highway 28. Newry turned the lumbering vehicle towards town and thought of Claire and the boys.

He thought of all his children on old Number Six. Their new day would be breaking soon enough.

16.

Recycling Center

KENNETH YAWNS AS HE inserts the key into the padlock and swings back the wide gate. With sweeping right turns, seven pickup trucks enter the large parking lot. Near dawn on the fourth day of Christmas, the dump at the end of Hickory Hollow Road reopens at 7:00 after the brief holiday lull.

Recycling bins for colored glass, triangularly coded plastic, tin cans, and old magazines line the far end of the lot, but the trucks—idling outside the fence for the last fifteen minutes—pass through the gate and angle leftward in what resembles rehearsed synchronicity, slowly backing into numbered parking spaces perpendicular to a giant metallic funnel easily capable of receiving tons of trash. So many bags fill the truck beds that each vehicle resembles Santa's sleigh burdened with mounds of shiny gifts, the rising sun glancing off the plastic in soft rays of color.

Five men and two women emerge from the truck cabs in slow motion—the caffeine not yet firing morning senses—and lower the rear gates of their vehicles with accompanying loud squeaks and abrupt thuds. They climb into respective truck beds and begin to arc the trash bags skyward towards the wide and receptive funnel.

Kenneth enters his small office wedged into the corner of the lot, blows on arthritic fingers, and gives thanks for the new coffee machine that he'd programmed on Christmas Eve to begin its magic in tandem with the opening of the entrance gate that morning on The Feast of the Slaughter of the Holy Innocents, a day he still observes on the liturgical calendar, which commemorates the deaths of all boys under two years executed upon the birth of Jesus by a paranoid King Herod. He will take delight throughout the day in greeting visitors to the landfill with the words, "Happy Slaughter of the Innocents Day!" All but one will stare back at him with eyes signaling they'll come no closer.

Through a tiny window, Kenneth marvels at all the bags in mid-air and then watches the path of a single bag as it leaves a released fist, rises towards an apex, and gives way to gravity. Rarely have any of the bags collided in all Kenneth's observations of the odd Dance of the Polyethylene.

A retired pastor, Kenneth tries to think of a Christmas hymn that might match the strange ballet of the airborne refuse and finally settles upon "Go Tell It on the Mountain," which he begins to hum between sips of coffee. He briefly thinks of Eunice McJunkin, the crotchety crone and organist in his last congregation who could barely scale the steep steps to the choir loft. Eunice played even the most familiar hymns at an agonizingly grinding pace.

The pastor consciously quickens his humming and scans the distant mountains of northeast Georgia and several visible peaks near the North Carolina state line, and again probes an old worry concerning the long-term effects of leaching landfills on the surrounding topography. Kenneth wonders what, exactly, disposable communities like his are "going and telling" these beautiful mountains. Over the hills and everywhere.

Expectant crows caw in the chill of the morning, looping around the landfill and biding their time for the discarded excess of the season. Kenneth wore a breathing mask over his nose last July to soften the acrid stench, a methane stew rising from the expansive acreage. The winter cold in the foothills of South Carolina, below freezing the last four nights, blessedly veils most of the December odor.

*

When Kenneth retired from the ministry two years ago at the age of sixty-two, he'd had enough. He told Doris, his wife, that he felt "saturated by woe" and couldn't stomach one more senseless death. Stillborn babies, teenage car wrecks, and the ravages of chemotherapy had all taken their toll with parishioners he'd loved and accompanied with presence and prayer.

Standing before the congregation on Sunday mornings and sharing the long list of needs for the church's prayer eventually made him feel like an empty ghost ship moving through life with nobody steering. The kids were gone now and expenses seemed manageable. With Doris's modest pension from teaching school and his retirement income from denominational

headquarters, they'd make it. He spent most of the first six months of retirement sitting in a chair and staring at a television screen framed by two
stocking feet raised on his old recliner.

Doris told him one afternoon in the marriage counselor's office that
she finally felt free enough to live her own life after following him around
to various parishes for thirty-five years. "There's no other man," she said.
"But I hope to find one." Kenneth never bothered to ask what she meant
by that. She volunteered to move out and didn't ask for a single thing extra
in the divorce settlement, where their assets were roughly divided equally.
These days, the only bits of information he hears about Doris are through
his children. She'd moved to Florida and had no intentions of moving any
further north ever again.

It became clear after a few months that Kenneth needed a job. Not so
much for the money. He needed something to do. The ad in the newspaper mentioned recycling and the word seemed to fit just about everything
about him that needed attention. The word even seemed to have theological
overtones and that connection surprisingly pleased him. He tore out the
ad and drove down to the county public works office at the Town Hall on
North Main Street.

*

The first few times his former parishioners saw their erstwhile pastor
working the magic of trash compaction at the landfill, they seemed genu-
inely surprised.

Never at a loss for words, Horace Peabody, who always sat four pews
back on the left side of the pulpit, told Kenneth he'd heard about the divorce. "I was sad and everything and prayed a couple times for you both
until I forgot about it, but I shore never thought you'd need some old smelly
job like this 'un. But come to think of it, everybody at the church used to
bring you the trash in their lives all the time, am I right? It makes some
sense that we still can. Get it? You followin' me?"

Horace, with several rolls of belly fat, laughed so hard that he almost
fell over the low railing that guarded the large metallic funnel. "Good to
see you, padre," he said, recovering. "I'll look for you next week. That is, if
you're still here. Adios, amigo."

Horace climbed into the cab of his red Silverado, fishtailed a bit on some loose gravel beyond the gate, and sounded an obnoxious horn that loudly resembled the happy retort of a train engine whistle.

It had become wonderfully liberating that Kenneth could now curse people he once had to tolerate. With a similar intensity to prayer, the pastor shouted a word across the empty parking lot that rhymed with the red vehicle that crested the hill on Hickory Hollow Road and disappeared.

*

The interviewer at the public works office downtown, Matt Turner, happened to be Doris's second cousin on her mother's side of the family. "I still don't know what got into Doris. The whole family's still pretty baffled by her leaving you for the Sunshine State. Guess you just don't know some people, even family."

Kenneth stared back at Matt for a few seconds until the silence felt uncomfortable and finally realized he was supposed to say something.

"Yeah, guess not," he said.

"Look, you've got the job if you want it," Matt said. "You're honestly the first person who's been in here asking about it and the position's been open for at least two weeks. I need to warn you, though. The last fella who took this job worked it almost five years until he couldn't stand it any longer. Something about his *old-factories* going haywire. That's your sense of smell, right? Seems like that'd be a blessing, if you ask me. He was sorta mad about the whole thing and we're now mired in a worker's comp case that's getting some attention down in Columbia, but why would a man want to quit *after* his smeller went haywire? Seems like you'd just be starting on a lucky career at the landfill if your nostrils weren't working properly."

Kenneth became aware of an odor in the room that smelled like someone had recently passed gas. From previous family reunions, Kenneth knew Matt had a good sense of humor and he wondered for a moment if his interviewer was making some sort of warped joke or perhaps darkly testing him for the rigors ahead.

*

Kenneth opened the gate on the morning of the Feast of Epiphany. There were no trucks waiting. He stood for a moment in the cold parking lot and watched a bank of stars in the darkened western sky. A meteor streaked low, flared, and died. He stood still for several minutes, looking up, until turning in the opposite direction to watch the rising sun slowly brighten the far horizon.

He emptied the recycling bins into larger dumpsters from yesterday's meager haul and walked toward his office at the corner of the lot. Just before reaching the waiting coffee, Kenneth thought he heard a child's voice from the far end of the landfill.

Kenneth didn't hear from his own children much anymore. They seemed to side with their mother in most things and, now in their late twenties and early thirties, weren't shy about voicing their contempt for all the moves they had to endure with their father's latest "call from God." He never tried to argue back. A move to a new place is tough on kids. He wondered if they'd ever forgive him.

Many years ago he tried to explain to his youngest son, Randy, a call to a new congregation in South Carolina, which would necessitate a family move from their home in Virginia. Kenneth could still hear Randy's angry and tearful sixth-grade voice: "Well, if God's callin' you, Dad, I want you to tell him to shut up!"

Just as Kenneth reached inside the warmth of the office to turn on the overhead light, he thought he heard the child's voice again. This time it sounded closer. The landfill was not near any neighborhoods. Who'd want to build a home downwind from such a place?

Kenneth mixed his coffee and read the local county paper, only a ten-minute commitment even in a busy news week. He pondered a single psalm from the Bible, a morning discipline for many decades, reflecting upon the 139th and an inescapable God who apparently had "searched and known" the writer whose days were numbered by God "when none of them as yet existed."

The pastor hoped God also knew his own flawed intentions so well, but many days Kenneth honestly wondered how the deity kept track of so many people. It seemed easy enough to hide amidst all the discarded garbage in a landfill, even from the gaze of God.

Kenneth poured more coffee into a large mug, pulled on his coat to check the parking lot, and almost knocked over a small boy who'd apparently been standing quietly just inside the office doorway for the last few minutes.

*

When Kenneth returned from checking the landfill parking lot, finally escaping an extended and rather heated conversation with Cory Dredger, a gap-toothed octogenarian who again failed to understand why used motor oil couldn't be dumped in a hole in his backyard "like my daddy done since 1942," the little boy was sitting at the office desk, still sipping a cup of hot chocolate Kenneth had mixed from an old packet of powdered Swiss Miss he'd found in a cabinet.

"Glad to see you're warming up a bit, young man," Kenneth said. "Tell me where you live so I can call your family."

"Done told you," said the little boy. "Don't have no family. I been livin' here in the landfill for awhile now. And my name's Larry, not Harry. I'm almost twelve, if you're wonderin'."

Kenneth thought the little boy, barely over four feet tall, looked a couple years younger than that. "So, you've been living right here? Out here in the cold in the middle of all this garbage? I don't mean to doubt you, Larry. But we need to establish something here from the start of our friendship. And I do want to be your friend. There's no lying at my landfill. How in the world have you been living here?"

There was something about Larry that seemed oddly familiar. Kenneth racked his brain, trying to recall if they'd met somewhere before.

The boy looked around the room. He checked the clock, looked back at the door, and went to the window to make sure the plastic bags were in the air and no one was heading towards the office. "Okay, I'll tell you. But you have to promise not to tell nobody. Promise?"

Kenneth looked at Larry and promised, and simultaneously recalled the promises he'd made to his own children, knowing he eventually broke some of them.

"We need to wait for the lot out yonder to clear," said Larry. "You don't have any secret hidden camera under your coat, do ya?"

*

When Kenneth was a little boy living in Greenwood, his parents, Fred and Esther, went out to a movie one January night and never made it home. Kenneth always wondered about the name of the movie they went to see and could have probably phoned the old theatre, still in operation on the town square, but he never did.

On the way home after the movie, his mom and dad slid across a patch of black ice, rare in South Carolina, and hit a large oak tree. Fred died instantly. Esther stopped breathing three days later in the county hospital. Even after he went to live with his aunt and uncle, Kenneth would ride his bike out to the tree. He never lingered very long but often tried to detect a scar in the tree trunk from the car's impact. As he touched the old oak, Kenneth wondered how many rings might reveal the tree's age and what other secrets it might hold.

His friend, Donny, told him once that the tree was "the same one they used to lynch niggers, back in the day." Kenneth believed his friend and would look up in the large limbs of the tree and imagine a rope and dangling noose as he touched the bark. He often said prayers at the tree for his parents and for others whose lives may have ended there.

Not long after his parents died, Kenneth began to imagine the day when he might become a pastor. There were things the minister said at his mom and dad's funeral and other things the man said at Aldersgate Methodist on Sunday mornings that Kenneth didn't understand or downright didn't believe.

The whole idea of God having "a purpose" for an icy accident just didn't make any sense at all. It wasn't such a wide stretch from having a purpose for the accident's outcome to actually causing the accident itself. "Can you imagine that God may have very much needed your mom and dad in heaven, Kenneth?" Even at age eleven, the little boy thought his pastor's suggestion was pretty crazy.

Kenneth would later discover that suffering can cause people to either reject God, or explore God more intensely. Kenneth chose the latter not only because of his prayers at the tree, but also because he had a dream one night in high school about another little boy who came to him for help, walking through a field of bones.

*

Larry looked back at Kenneth when they were halfway down a path through the landfill and completely out of sight of the large metallic funnel. "You'd better let me take your hand for awhile," said the little boy. "It gets sort of tricky up ahead."

Kenneth stifled a low laugh. He'd walked this path dozens of times to check on one thing or another, most recently to accompany a state hydrologist collecting a quarterly water sample from the creek that flowed along the eastern edge of the property and eventually emptied into the Chattooga River. But he accepted Larry's suggestion anyway.

He thought of his son, Randy. It was nice to hold the hand of a little boy again. Kenneth noticed that the boy's hands seemed rougher than other kids he knew of a similar age. He also felt what seemed like a scar in the center of Larry's palm and began to wonder why he hadn't called social services right away back at the landfill office.

The pastor already knew that January masked the otherwise-pungent smells of the place, but this particular morning seemed almost free of anything malodorous. Instead, a steady hint of the scent of bloodroot—one of the first wildflowers of the spring, still a couple months away from appearing in the Carolina hills—caused him to scan beyond the creek for blooms on the opposite bank where he'd noticed a stand of flowers last March. Only a dusting of snow now clung there.

"Do you smell that?" Kenneth asked his guide.

"Smell what?" Larry replied without looking back.

"Those flowers. It's been awhile since I took botany back in my college days, but I could swear I smell bloodroot. One of our earliest flowers in the spring here in the South Carolina mountains with eight white petals or so. Yellow center; only lasts a few days. You know it?"

Larry stopped in the path and turned around to look at his new friend. "Yeah, I know that one. Just wait. You're gonna be surprised. Keep followin' me." The little boy was smiling. This time he was the one who almost laughed.

*

When Kenneth first started working at the landfill, new to the machinery and his daily tasks, there was almost a rather gruesome incident. The previous day had been crazy busy. Mondays and Fridays were usually the worst, but this was a Thursday and for some reason more trucks of trash appeared that afternoon than recorded during any single day all year on the landfill clipboard log.

When five o'clock rolled around, Kenneth was bone tired and decided to leave several bags of garbage in the bottom of the metallic funnel. He locked the gate and made a mental note to deal with the bags first thing the following morning.

He arrived at the landfill earlier than normal on Friday, wanting to clear the powerful maw of the compactor before the crowd surged in, preparing for the weekend ahead. Clemson had a home football game the next day. He didn't blame people for wanting to clean out their homes before the kickoff and the next round of refuse that would undoubtedly accumulate in the dens of the varied Tiger faithful.

Kenneth himself was a man of rather tidy order. He liked things neat and in place, so the first thing he did that morning, even before his coffee, was to flip on the compactor breaker switch in the landfill office (a security measure), walk back to the right of the railing in the empty lot, and push the red button inside the wooden box that he'd just unlocked with a small key.

A noisy piece of machinery, the compactor began to engage yesterday's leftover garbage bags. The pastor always winced at the sounds of crunching cans, deflating plastic milk jugs, and the collision of items that God surely wanted kept asunder in any sane ecology. Coffee would soon soothe these foreign sounds not fit for anyone's ears.

With his hand on the office doorknob, Kenneth heard a repeated and panicked scraping sound from the bowels of the compactor that easily sliced through the usual din of noise. Something with claws was trying to climb the angled walls of the funnel. He was closer to the breaker box than the red button. Within seconds, there was silence.

Kenneth cautiously peered over the railing. The light that illumined the landfill lot before sunrise did not quite reach the bottom, but he could make out the shape anyway. Breathing hard in the middle of torn bags of garbage at the bottom of the funnel was a small exhausted bear cub, looking up at him with eyes filled with panic. Kenneth tried not to think of the awful sound he'd almost heard had the machine not been stopped in time. "Well, hello there, little fella," he said. "You must have been hungry."

Richard Morris, his DNR friend and a former parishioner, arrived within thirty minutes of Kenneth's call, still before the seven o'clock opening of the landfill. Richard was in charge of the county bear population and also mowed a few lawns on the side. He had a special truck for relocating bears.

"I'd say about a thousand," said Richard, in answer to Kenneth's question about the county bear numbers. "About 90 percent of my nuisance bear calls involve little guys like this one. Adolescent males. They get pushed out of the den around this age and have no idea what to do. It'd be like you telling your twelve-year-old to pack his bags and hit the road. They're just not ready, but that's the way of the wild, Rev."

After Richard departed with his rescued cargo, Kenneth opened the gate for four trucks waiting outside. They all said hello as the trash bags began their mid-air dance, but nobody asked about the DNR truck that had just departed the landfill.

*

Larry led Kenneth across the fairly wide creek on a series of stones that somebody had placed since his recent trip there with the hydrologist. Each stone looked far too heavy for any little boy to manage. They climbed up the opposite bank to the top of a low ridge and an old fence line now marked only by an occasional wooden post. The patchy snow had melted quickly in the morning sun and the pastor noticed several bluets, an early spring wildflower oddly blooming in January, popping up through the moist earth.

Several worn trails fanned out in various directions into the pasture. From the height of the ridge, Kenneth could tell they all led back to a point just out of view, descending slightly. Larry took a trail to the left. "This isn't the quickest way," he said. "But it's my favorite."

Kenneth couldn't have said how far or long they walked. It didn't seem to matter. As he followed the little boy, a sense of contentment flowed over him that Kenneth hadn't felt in a long time. Once or twice he thought of his duties back at the landfill, but mostly he thought of his parents, Doris, and the children, and the mistakes he'd made in the parishes he'd served. Even the worst of the memories seemed to find a certain peace in this pasture with this strange child who'd wandered into his life.

Kenneth noticed he'd removed his winter coat. "You won't be needin' that for awhile," Larry said. "But maybe we can lie down here for a bit and take a rest."

The pastor spread his coat out on the path. It was big enough for both of them to lie back and look up. Neither the man nor the boy spoke for a length of time that eluded Kenneth's ability to measure. Clouds floated by. Red-winged blackbirds called and played tag back and forth across the meadow.

"Pretty, ain't it?" Larry rose and resumed walking without waiting to see if Kenneth was following along behind.

"Is this where you live?" asked Kenneth.

"Yeah, most of the time."

"What do you eat? Who takes care of you?"

"We're almost there. Just enjoy the walk."

*

One of the reasons Kenneth eventually enjoyed working at the landfill was people could bring garbage there and leave it. He knew his patrons saw nothing more in their weekly deposits than convenience, but somebody paid to make Sunday morning connections between the sacred and mundane saw a liberating unburdening in the messy work he oversaw. Down the funnel, push a button, and goodbye garbage.

Kenneth knew it wasn't that easy. The garbage had to go somewhere after the compactor did its thing. But there was something appealing about presiding over what felt like an emptying of temporal concern and worry.

He never pushed the red button when anyone else was around; didn't want any local teenagers to know what was in the wooden box high and to the right of the railing, but he suspected they already knew.

Once, on a slow morning, a woman he'd never seen before drove up in a brand-new Cadillac and emptied the contents of her trunk one bag at a time, slowly, into the funnel. When the trunk was cleaned out, she stood at the railing for at least five minutes, looking down. Kenneth watched her through the office window and finally walked out to see if she needed anything else.

"What happens to it now?" she asked.

Kenneth patiently explained the process. The woman asked him a question. For what would be the first and only time during his work at the landfill, Kenneth unlocked the wooden box and allowed someone else to push the red button that engaged the gears of the compactor.

She needed a small stepladder from the office. After descending the couple steps with Kenneth's assistance, she asked for a moment alone.

Kenneth couldn't resist looking through the small office window. Oblivious to the possibility of any tears in her panty hose, the woman knelt in front of the funnel on the pavement with her eyes closed and head bowed until a truck loudly entered the lot.

Gripping the railing, she slowly rose from her knees and drove away.

*

"We're here," said the boy.

Kenneth hadn't noticed coming upon the large tree that now stood in their path in the meadow.

"This is where you live?"

"Like I said, most of the time."

"I know we just walked here. But I've never seen this place. Where are we exactly in relation to the dump?"

Larry didn't answer, but started climbing the tree's branches, laughing and swinging higher, until he was almost out of sight from the ground.

There was something about the tree that seemed familiar to Kenneth. He walked around the wide periphery of the trunk, out to the line separating sun and shade, and looked up again through the crisscrossing limbs for the boy. A slight breeze blew across the upper leaves.

Kenneth touched the bark of the tree—an old oak whose age was anybody's guess. There was an instant and old kinship in the touch. He walked completely around the tree in both directions, never losing contact with the trunk with one hand, then the other.

A crease in the bark of the tree stopped his hand at about the height of his waist, a long vertical raised section of the old trunk that seemed almost grown over from the many layers of bark, but had once surely been a much deeper gash. For the first time in many years, he remembered a child on a bicycle who pedaled out to a tree to look up and pray.

"Did you find it?" called down Larry.

"Find what?"

"The scar. There's thousands of 'em in this here old tree. Millions maybe. But I suspect you located the one you needed to find. That's why you're here."

*

These days at the landfill everybody knows Kenneth's name. He's been a fixture long enough that people bring him Christmas cookies every December. One woman even surprised him with a gift card last week from

168

Starbuck's in Seneca "so that you won't have to drink that dreadful excuse for coffee the county buys for you."

Horace Peabody, as a joke, even brought him a sign with the words "Rev's Dump" burned into the wood with a nice cursive flair. It now hangs permanently on Kenneth's office door.

Occasionally, people show up with renegade items for disposal, clearly outside state regulations. "Now you realize I can't take just anything and make it go away!" the pastor tells them.

He always smiles as the words come out of his mouth and thinks of Larry. Kenneth hasn't seen the little boy since crossing back over the creek that day on the return to the landfill after visiting the tree. They walked over the stones, Kenneth looked back, and the little boy wasn't there. The sheriff's office contacted Kenneth several times after he called, but nobody fitting Larry's description was ever reported missing.

"There are worse jobs than working at a dump in December," Kenneth thinks as he looks out the window of his office at bundled visitors whose breath forms several small vapor clouds in front of the metallic funnel.

He again wonders what Christmas carol might accompany the swirling dance of the airborne garbage bags. Kenneth starts to hum "Brightest and Best," one of his favorites, remembering the bright star on the morning of the child's arrival.

The pastor sings softly in time with the bags.

"Dawn on our darkness and lend us thine aid. Star of the east, the horizon adorning . . ."

Two bags collide in mid-air. The song trails off.

"Guide," he prays, smiling.

CPSIA information can be obtained
at www.ICGtesting.com
Printed in the USA
LVHW110014240320
651002LV00005B/1657

9 781532 675515